BOOK 1
OF THE MODERATOR CHRONICLES

THE MODERATORS

LILAH SOUZA

COPYRIGHT PAGE

Table of Contents

PROLOGUE

He had been wrong. This wasn't anything like the movies he had seen. This wasn't a game. It was kill or be killed. He now knew that he had to fight back, terrified as he was. Suddenly, his arms started to glow a brilliant pure white.

CHAPTER 1

Jason growled, slamming his keyboard. Typh had walked them right into this fight, and it wasn't looking good.

"Adonus! I need some help!" Typh shouted into his headset to Jason.

"Don't worry, I'm on your six, Typh! Where the hell's Meowth? They were supposed to be up here ages ago."

"I'm coming! I was trying to figure out how the special attacks work," MeowthDatsWrong replied.

"I guess we should've picked an easier event," Typhlosion_L0ver grumbled.

"Shut up! You guys know I'm new at this!"

"Hey, Adonus! You're being attacked from behind!" he heard someone shout into his headset.

Boom!

Before Jason could do anything, his shoulders tightened as his teammates were picked off one by one around him. A moment later, all he could see was a giant ball of fire honing in on him and his avatar's health plummeted to 0. Stupid frame rate. He could've easily dodged it if his crusty four-year-old laptop could handle the updated graphics of the game.

"Crap," he sighed, slumping over in his desk.

Jason's ears were heating up from the hours he'd spent wearing his headset and his throat was dry. What he needed now was a nice, cool glass of water.

He walked down the moonless corridor of his home. His body jittered as though a blanket of bitter wind had wrapped around him. Like he wasn't alone. Like something was out there. As Jason made his way into the kitchen, his breath snagged. Something flickered in the corner of his eye.

His eyes wheeled in the direction of a small girl in a mud-brown cloth dress, almost identical in hue to the vines draping over her bruised face, and barely hiding the varying shades of red grazes across her arms and legs.

"H-hey there, little girl … Are you lost?" he asked.

The girl turned, her chin drooped, and silently shook her head, making Jason's stomach drop slightly.

Then the girl lifted her head up to reveal a face covered with gruesome, bloodied lacerations from her eye sockets to her mouth, which grew wider and wider until they reached her cheekbone. Jason backed away from the girl and ran to his mother's bedroom.

With what little breath he had left, he pushed the door wide open. "Mom! Mom! There's a girl in the hallway! Her face is all cut up!"

"What? Not this again, Jason. I thought you had outgrown that years ago. It's late. You're just seeing things. Go back to bed," his mother mumbled drowsily and fell back asleep.

Fine, he thought. *I'll take care of it myself.* He fumed as he rushed back down the hallway to check on the girl.

Silence.

"But … but … I could've sworn …" He searched the hallway for a sign of the girl. No luck.

He rushed back into his room and dug through his dresser. Since Jason was a kid, he could see spirits but was usually too scared to talk to them. He would just write descriptions of the spirits down in a journal and wonder about their stories. To prepare for whatever might come his way, Jason had begun keeping journal entries of *all* the weird stuff that happened that couldn't be explained. He charted every instance of the alien and bizarre that appeared in the news, social media, or word of mouth. He faithfully logged them in his notebook, noting the precise date and hour of their occurrence. In the past couple of weeks, these sightings had been happening way more frequently.

The entry on the previous page read:

Two young women ice skating on the lake at

Central Park. They were dressed in old period clothing. Appeared to be sisters, possibly the Van der Voort sisters.

On the next page he wrote: *Sunday, September 9. 11:00 p.m. Little girl with olive skin, dark hair, wearing strange dress. Possibly a Native American slave girl. Possibly kidnapped and beaten to death. Did not appear to be hostile.*

When he finished writing, he put the notebook back in his drawer and slumped into his bed. The air in his room suddenly chilled to the point that he wasn't thirsty anymore.

*   *   *

After school, Jason strolled down the school hallway to get a drink from the water fountain. As he leaned over, he felt someone shove his face right into the fountain, water shooting up his mouth and nose.

The burn was real. Jason's nostrils inflamed and he went into a coughing fit before swiveling in the other direction to see who did it. A statuesque boy and a petite girl, both with shaggy obsidian hair and the same black-and-gold uniform as Jason's, giggled down the hall trying—and failing—to look innocent. The boy, however, had on a leather jacket and expensive-looking sneakers contrasting with Jason's standard-issue school sweater and black Vans. As the boy and girl disappeared down the hallway, he saw the flash of a moment from a day at his previous school—a group of boys pointing and mocking him and calling him "Greek Geek," a girl's face curdling into itself at the sight of him.

And here he thought coming to a school in Manhattan where nobody knew him would change things. Seemed like more of the same.

He shook it off and made a left down to the double doors of the gymnasium leading to the back of the building where Archery Club was being held. He walked outside past the Fencing Club's court. He stopped for a moment, scanned the court, then the benches.

And there he saw *her*.

Kalen Morrigan was tapping her foot waiting for her turn to spar with a look of intense determination in her emerald-green eyes. Her sherbet-orange hair was tied back in a slick, neat ponytail, dangling over and overshadowing her bulky white fencing uniform, while her bright green eyes popped out from under her messy bangs. Kalen was called. She donned her helmet and vest, then carried her foil sword onto the line looking over at the coach for the start signal.

The bout started with the opponent leaning into Kalen with the tip of their foil, while Kalen jutted back and around them. When the opponent plunged their foil toward her stomach, she swiftly dodged it and vigorously swung at her adversary.

Kalen honed in on the opponent and sent them staggering with a barrage of strikes. Jason watched as Kalen thundered towards her opponent, her weapon flashing from side to side. She extended her arm into a lunge, her ponytail swinging up as she hit.

"Point!" the coach shouted.

The opponent got back up to fight again, this time seeming to try a different approach. They began to circle to the right around Kalen, who kept vigilant, her foil still held high. But then the opponent faked her out and jabbed left, making Kalen turn around and the foil land on her left shoulder.

"Point!" the coach shouted again.

The two fencers got back into center and began again, Kalen gripping her foil tighter than usual. This time, she went for it before the opponent could even hold their foil steady. In the blink of an eye, a cry broke out. The opponent was on the ground, clutching their side, while the coach rushed over to stop Kalen.

The fencing coach leaped in between the two fencers, motioned to Kalen's face and gestured to the bench. Whenever she was fencing, Kalen tended to get lost in the heat of the battle and go a little overboard. Jason couldn't help but feel bad, watching her sulk on the bench.

"Hey, Jay; who *is* that? Do you know her

from somewhere?" a female club mate of Jason's came up to him and asked.

"That's Kalen. I definitely wouldn't want to get into a fencing match with her." Jason smiled nervously.

"Same here, dude." His club mate shuddered.

"C'mon Walker, wipe that stupid grin off your face and get to practice!" their archery coach interrupted.

When Jason turned to see that his club mate had already left him behind, he sighed, picked up his bow and arrow, and rushed to Archery Club to get ready for target practice.

*   *   *

Man! What did I do? Kalen thought. *All I did out there was give 110%! If you aren't giving 110% on your fencing, you're not trying hard enough.*

At least that's what her mother always said. A resigned sigh wisped through her lips as she looked at her opposition being slowly walked to the bench on the other side.

She shifted her gaze to the Archery Club next door, which the new kid, Jason, had joined when he came to the school last year. His choppy light brown hair and childlike hazel eyes reminded her of a puppy. But he was also kind of weird. One time in the hallway, he bumped into her and just started to mumble and walk away, which slightly irritated her. He could've at least apologized.

She'd also caught him looking at her while she practiced more times than she could count. Gage never stopped teasing her about him.

Another thing she didn't get about Jason was why he would ever pick a sport as lame as archery. It just didn't seem aggressive and competitive enough. Still, even though he wasn't the best archer in the group, he always did fairly well—at least from what she could tell—which earned her respect.

"Walker!" the archery coach squawked in Jason's direction.

She studied Jason as he walked over to a target carrying his bow and strapping a quiver full of arrows onto his shoulder.

Let's see if this guy is actually any good at this, she thought.

Kalen watched from across the dense shrubbery that separated the two clubs as Jason, alongside several other archers, lifted their bows and pulled back their arrows. Then she heard a loud gunshot that must have been deafening from where the archers were standing.

Before she could collect herself, arrows fired, making sharp thudding sounds onto the targets. She scanned the field for Jason's arrow. She shook her head, balling her gloved hands into angry fists on his behalf. Mere inches from the bullseye. So close!

*   *   *

On the other end of the hedge, Jason gave a small but proud smile. So close! When he was just starting out, he couldn't even hit the target. Everyone would laugh about him after practice. Everyone except his friend Dimitria. Dimitria was another transfer student, except she was from Queens. So they sort of bonded over the fact that they were basically the only "foreigners" at Dwayne Whitewood High.

Dimitria held up her hand and instinctively Jason high-fived her. She smiled and said, "Nice job, Jay! Look who's actually hitting close to the bullseye this time!"

"You too, Di! Oh, next time, aim further up," he teased back, pointing at her arrow, which was just below his, earning him a playful shove on the shoulder.

"And to think not that long ago, I was the one giving you the pointers. Don't go getting too much better than me now!" Dimitria said, as she began to put her gear away and head toward the lockers.

"Hey, so movie night tonight. You down?"

Jason asked her as he put some of the arrows he collected into his quiver.

"Sure man, I'll go with you. I don't really have anything better to do right now, anyway." Dimitria smirked.

"Oh, thanks," Jason said, drawing out the word. "So that's why you're tagging along with me. Not because it's like our weekly tradition or anything but because you have nothing better to do. I see how it is." Jason shoved her teasingly. He felt a rush of happiness. Yeah, there were dumb kids like the ones who shoved his face into the water fountain at Whitewood High. But there were also kids like Dimitria, and Kalen.

"Let's hop to it, then. I'm craving their nachos today."

*   *   *

After fencing practice was over, Kalen arrived at the locker room, left shoulder a little sore from the sparring match. How could she have let herself get blindsided like that?

She got dressed and mimed carving a rune onto her palm with her fingernail. In an instant, she moved her shoulder again and breathed a sigh of relief. Good as new. She did this every time she got hurt in Fencing Club. Her mother taught her about the runes to keep her safe.

When she walked out of the locker room, an underclassman walked up to her, startling her a bit.

"Hey," the guy said haltingly, as though he was about to give Kalen some bad news.

"Hey," she echoed back. "And you are …?"

"Giordano, from philosophy. So … what're you doing after fencing tonight?"

"Dunno, Giordano from philosophy. Probably just going home to study. Got that big test coming up."

Giordano nodded and gave one of those smiles that was tight and didn't really reach all the way to his eyes. "Right, right. What about the rest of the week?"

"Probably the same thing."

Giordano scrunched his face and tilted his head. "Really? Well, I was thinking of heading to the movies to see *The Exorcism of Mary Sue*. If you want, you could come with and we could get to know each other a little better."

She didn't have a lot of experience with this sort of thing, but even Kalen could tell where this was going. She nodded her head in realization and told him, "Listen, I'm not interested in dating. Never have been, don't think I ever will be."

Giordano scrunched his eyebrows. "You really expect me to believe you haven't felt that way about *anyone*? *Ever*?"

"That's about the size of it."

"Maybe you just haven't found your type? Maybe you'll come to find it if you keep an open—"

"Nope. I just really don't have a 'type,' okay?"

Giordano pursed his lips and nodded his head. Brushing past Kalen to get to the guys' locker room, he said, "Word of advice for the future: If you're gonna turn someone down, at least have the decency to be honest about why you're doing it."

"I ... *am* being hon—," Kalen started to say but the guy stormed into the locker room before she could finish her sentence.

Kalen stared at the closed door. She really was being honest with him. She had genuinely never felt attracted to anyone. She had done some research on the internet and found that there were lots of people like her, but most people she knew offline either didn't know about it or didn't believe in it. Giordano-from-philosophy did have a point, though. She could tell herself "Maybe I just haven't met the right person yet" each day until the day she died. And even when she died, maybe she just hadn't lived long enough to meet the right person. But she'd decided early on in high school that she wouldn't get caught up in maybes and would go after things she actually desired, which currently centered around getting that coveted law degree.

*   *   *

Gage sighed deeply as he waited in front of the school. He was supposed to wait there and meet up with Kalen. Heavy rock music blasted through his iPod as he sat on the steps, tapping his feet. No one had come out yet, but at least Kalen had texted saying she was on the way. Then a hand with black nail polish pulled his shaggy black hair back, while another pinched his nose, making him yelp.

"What was that for?" he asked Amelia, a petite Asian in thick black-rimmed glasses.

"I'm bored! When is she coming out already? I wanna go home," Amelia whined, continuing to pinch his nose.

"If you're so damn bored, why don't you go home? Or better yet, do something with your boyfriend, Sandro?" Gage retorted.

"Because I'm off work today and he isn't. And I ran out of manga at home …"

"Ugh, you know what? I can't blame you. I don't exactly wanna be sittin' around here myself."

"I don't get it. Why do you let Kalen order you around like that? Are you into her or something?" she teased.

Gage retreated into his hoodie, turning to hide his reddening face like a turtle hiding in its shell. "*Tch.* Gage Sato Samson don't let *nobody* order him around. She just texted me a minute ago sayin' practice was gonna be a bit longer. I don't go for uptight Type A personalities like her, anyway," he said, his Brooklyn accent thickening.

"Sure, you don't. Alright man, if it means that much to you …" Amelia chuckled. "Wait, *Sato*?"

"Hey, I'm half Japanese! Lay off!" Gage snapped.

Gage and Amelia waited several minutes when someone loudly knocked on the door, making Gage jump up. It was Kalen. Hopefully neither Amelia or Kalen noticed him jumping. Real cool.

When Kalen opened the door and walked out, Gage recovered and said, "So, how was it?"

"It was alright." Kalen said. Amelia was sputtering, obviously trying not to laugh. Kalen looked at her in confusion.

"Let's go!" Gage said, walking quickly ahead.

*   *   *

Trudging through a cavernous, poorly lit Manhattan subway, Kalen looked at Gage. "How's Beatrice getting home?" Gage's foster sister always tagged along with them, which Kalen didn't mind since she was so sweet.

"Don't worry; Beatrice has a car." Then he raised his brows at her and said, "It's Friday night;

let's go to somewhere fun, like the movies! I'll hit up Beatrice, Amelia, and Sandro and we can all see that cool looking exorcism movie!"

"Sounds fun!" Kalen said. She put her hand on his shoulder. "You don't mind paying this time, do you, Gage? You do owe me for the last trip to the movies."

She gave him a wry smile, letting him know she was half joking.

Gage tightened his lips and focused his eyes literally everywhere else. "Ugh, fine," he muttered.

The train pulled in, a cloud of smoke permeating the ground floor and giving off the faint smell of sewage—and what Gage thought was McDolan's ketchup. Soon, they met up with Amelia. The group got onto the train, along with dozens of other busy or zoned out Manhattanites, all packed inside like tinned fish. Kalen and Amelia were able to find seats while Gage was stuck hanging onto the poles. He sighed in resignation and started to space out.

Then Kalen's eyes locked on something out the window. She jumped, bumping into a girl just behind her trying to read her book. Gabe and the other passengers turned and stared at her.

Gage asked, "What is it, Kalen?"

"Nothing." She was leaning forward, still staring out the window.

"Okay, then. Don't scare me like that, man

…"

Gage shrugged and continued zoning out.

On the train car behind them, Jason turned to the window and saw what he thought were multiple handprints pressed against it. He jumped, bumping into the old lady next to him, who whacked him in his calf with a cane. He checked the window again and saw nothing but black and subway cables.

What the hell was that?

Then he stopped himself and shook his head.

No. It's like my mom always tells me. I'm just imagining it ...

As the track stretched on and on, outside the setting sun sunk farther and farther until darkness enveloped the city sky.

CHAPTER 2

The group arrived at a movie theater in Times Square, a cultural rite of passage for anyone growing up around or visiting NYC. Now that it was nighttime, the crisp autumn air had become a painful arctic blast, especially when having to maneuver around massive crowds and slow-walking tourists. When Sandro finally did show—and after waiting in a shivering huddle in the ticket line—the group scurried inside the movie theater to buy tickets for *The Exorcism of Mary Sue*. After buying some popcorn and snacks, they went inside the room where the movie was playing and scanned it for good seats. The room was packed, but they did manage to find a couple of good seats around the middle. Sandro, a tall, tan Brazilian boy, grabbed a blushing Amelia by the upper waist and pulled her over to a pair of seats in the center.

"Hey! Hands off!" Amelia whispered.

"What? Are you saying you don't wanna sit together?" asked Sandro.

"It's not that, I just … ugh! You're so embarrassing sometimes!"

Kalen asked, "Hey, what about Beatrice?"

"Trix said she was gonna sit this one out. Said she was pretty tired."

"Well, I mean, it is a school night," Kalen shrugged.

Kalen went over to the seat next to Amelia and Sandro. Gage was behind her about to turn to the last seat next to hers.

Kalen sighed with a measure of exasperation and motioned for him to sit. She didn't need him to treat her like a baby.

The movie began with a normal young girl named Mary Sue playing tag with her friends in a barn. Then, in the middle of the game, she suddenly stops moving, tenses up, and starts writhing on the floor in pain.

The other kids cry out, "Mary Sue! Mary Sue! Are you okay, Mary Sue?"

Then, when the curly blonde turned to answer, she let out an ear-piercing screech that made everyone in the audience jump from their seats.

Kalen got splashed with buttered popcorn from some schmuck sitting in front of her. It was like getting pelted with little spitballs that left a thick spot of grease everywhere they landed.

As she pawed the buttery popcorn off of herself, the kid smiled bashfully. "My bad."

Kalen scowled when she realized it was Jason sitting next to one of his archery buddies. That guy kept giving her reasons to hate him.

She shook her head and got up to go to the

bathroom and clean herself up. She could hear Gage snickering from behind her, so she turned around and gave him a hard, violent glare, and he looked away, feigning innocence.

*   *   *

Dimitria turned to him and motioned to his clothes, "Uhh, Jay? You've got popcorn *all over you.*"

Jason looked down and groaned. He hadn't realized what a mess he'd made. Dimitria saluted him off as he got up to go get himself cleaned up.

Then he spotted Kalen heading in the same direction. Maybe he could at least apologize.

He ghosted in Kalen's direction, inciting her to stare daggers—or rapiers—at him.

"Hey. I'm sorry about your top …," he managed to say.

"I would hope so. It was a birthday gift. A particularly expensive one," she groused.

Jason's insides sunk. "O-oh …," he stammered.

She shook her head and her gaze softened a bit. "I've seen you at the gymnasium. Archery Club, right?"

Jason felt his heart skip a beat. *She'd* been watching *him*?!

"You're not bad," she said nonchalantly.

"Thanks! Fencing Club, right? You're not too bad yourself!" Jason said, trying his best to mirror her nonchalance.

Kalen eyes bulged and her ears went red

Oh no. Maybe he'd taken the nonchalant thing too far. "Uh, Kalen? Are you okay?"

"Oh! Yeah, I'm fine. It's nothing."

"Well, it was nice talking to you. Enjoy the movie!" Jason said, attempting cheerfulness now.

"Yeah, you too," Kalen said as she followed Jason down the hallway to the restrooms, staying several feet behind him.

Jason went into the boys' bathroom and turned on the faucet on the sink in front of him. He grabbed some paper towels, soaked them in water, and began to wipe his face. He couldn't believe he had gotten so jumpy over the movie that he'd dumped his popcorn, on Kalen of all people!

He smacked himself on the forehead and muttered to himself, "Ugh! You *idiot!*"

A man using the sink next to him said, "First date? I've so been there, man."

"She's not my date … I mean, I do sort of *want* her to be, though. Like that'll happen now ..."

The man just shrugged and wished him good luck as he walked out the door. He probably knew Jason was a lost cause.

After Jason rinsed his hands and turned off the faucet, he heard a loud thump that he could have sworn came from the ceiling. He looked up and saw nothing. He shrugged it off and checked his face in the mirror again. He stepped back from the mirror. Black smoke was permeating the restroom.

Ugh, really? Smoking in a movie theater bathroom? Wasn't that banned, like, decades ago?

Jason walked toward the door and reached for the handle. Then the lights went out. He jiggled the door handle, but it wouldn't budge. The room was a murky black. He felt as though he had been put into a dark oven or someone was breathing hot air down his neck, but the heat enveloped his whole body. He reached for his cellphone and turned on his flashlight app. When the bright light came on, he held the phone to the door to see if there was a way to force it open. His hands were shaking a little now.

Then he heard the shuffling of feet behind him, making him spin in the other direction.

He yelped at the gruesome face standing behind him.

It was what appeared to be a young girl, about preteen age, with pigtails, an evil, murderous glint in her eye, and a big, black cleaver for an appendage. The girl's hair was stringy and ink colored, and her skin gray, cracked, and rotten looking.

"What the …?"

He took a few steps back from this ghastly

looking girl when she let out an ear-shattering scream that blew her bangs away, revealing a manic, pallid, cracking visage and the dark abysses of her eyes. Jason jumped back and screamed, darting around her. The shadowy girl teleported in front of him, swinging her cleaver at him while laughing hysterically in a voice far too deep to belong to a girl her size.

Jason staggered to the sinks before catching a glimpse in the mirror of the girl's cleaver swinging toward his neck. He ducked. Before he knew it, he had slashes on the sleeves of his shirt, and spurts of blood were dripping from them.

There was no way in hell he was "just imagining" *this*.

The cleaver stuck to the wall for a moment, giving him the chance to run. He sprinted for the bathroom door, but just when he was about to touch the knob, the shadowy girl slashed him on the back with her cleaver. He fell to the floor, the girl standing over him ready to make the next strike.

He quickly braced his arms in front of him as a blocking reflex and rolled out of the way just as her massive cleaver dug into the tiled floor. The tiny girl somehow pulled out her weapon and swung it around as though it were as light as paper. He flinched as another swing came for him. Next thing he knew he was backed into a wall. Then something dawned on Jason; he had seen way too many of these types of movies to *not* know what to do next. Heck, he was supposed to be watching one right now. He ran to the sink, cupped some water into his hands, and started tossing it at the monstrous girl.

"The power of Christ compels you! The power of Christ compels you," he shouted.

He kept tossing more and more water at the girl, but she didn't even flinch; she just kept chuckling and flailing her weapon about dementedly.

Damn it ... What the hell do I do now?

He had been wrong. This *wasn't* anything like the movies. It wasn't a game either. It was kill or be killed. He now knew that he had to fight back, terrified as he was.

Suddenly, his arms started to glow visibly white. The brightness of the light sent the shadow girl staggering away in what seemed to be fear and pain.

"How am even I doing this?" he muttered as he got to his feet.

A glowing bow and arrow appeared in his hands. He grinned and walked closer to the girl. The girl backed further away from him the closer he got, looking like a cautious animal backing away from a lit torch.

As he approached her, he felt no guilt. An eye for an eye, and all that.

The shadow girl screamed in pain, then,

turning to Jason once more, suddenly disappeared. Jason scanned the room for her, and then jumped when a black hand touched his ankle. The girl smiled creepily, her dark eyes opened wide, and she raised her cleaver to Jason's leg. Suddenly, another glowing white weapon slashed through the girl's arm, severing it. The weapon was shaped like a sword; more specifically, a *rapier* fencing sword. Jason turned to see his red-headed crush kick the ghoul to the floor and pull him out of the fray.

"Kalen …? W-what's happening? Why is she ...? How are we …?"

"I'll explain later. For now, stay back. Your bow and arrow are useless from this range."

"O-okay …" Jason stepped away from her.

"Alright, ugly! You mess with *him* you have to answer to *me*!" Kalen declared. The shadow girl charged at her. Kalen jumped and drop-kicked her enemy to the wall. When Kalen landed, she hurled forward and slashed at the her with her sword.

Her rapier and the shadow girl's cleaver collided and sent them both flying backwards. Kalen landed on her feet, while the girl fell on her back. Kalen rushed up to the shadow girl and held her glowing blade to her neck.

"Who sent you, Shadowmonster?" she asked sharply.

Jason squinted his eyes. "*Shadowmonster?*"

"I won't tell you, Moderator," the shadow

girl sneered. Then, her mouth curled into an eerie ear-to-ear smirk and she kicked Kalen in the stomach, sending her falling back.

"Kalen!" Jason cried.

Kalen picked herself back up and smiled, lifting her rapier to shield herself.

She parried the creature's swings and then pierced her rapier into her stomach, but the shadow girl's cleaver stopped her, and then slashed Kalen's shoulder, though only slicing her shirt.

Kalen elbowed the shadow girl, then slashed her in the air while jumping unusually high and doing a spinning somersault. She kicked the shadow girl while still in the air, knocking the cleaver out of her hand. The cleaver hit the ground and disintegrated before their eyes. Then the shadow girl generated a dark orb from her hand, and out came another cleaver.

The shadow girl charged furiously at Kalen, who was charging at her, too. The two blades collided, and then both girls stepped back. The shadow girl charged again. Kalen dodged with a side step, and then began to make multiple jabs to the other girl's chest. Exactly how she had done it in fencing practice. Only five times as fast.

Only one thought kept echoing in Jason's mind: Where the *hell* did Kalen learn to fight like that?!

Kalen spun and struck the girl once more

with a stronger jab, and the shadow girl screamed and exploded into a puff of black smoke.

Kalen panted, out of breath from the fighting, and staggered over to Jason's limp body, who was nearly about to pass out from the amount of blood he had lost.

"Are you okay?" she asked in a concerned tone.

"Yeah," Jason replied. He couldn't help noticing how beautiful Kalen's face looked so close to his, and so worried about him.

"Uh, why're you looking at me like that?" she asked.

"Um … I … no reason," Jason replied, chuckling nervously.

Kalen summoned more of the glowing energy that her weapon had, though this time it was only a small orb and, he noticed, there was a strange glowing mark on her hand that hadn't been there a second ago. She spread the energy from the orb to Jason's wounds.

Jason was about to ask Kalen what she was doing, but she interrupted by saying, "Shhh, I'm healing you."

"Oh …" He could feel the heat rising in him from all over his body.

Kalen stepped away from him and said, "Hold still."

He did what she said, and soon the light

consumed his body. Slowly, steadily, the air around him started to buzz, vibrating louder and louder until every follicle on his head stood on end. When the glowing light faded, along with the mark on Kalen's hand, he peered at and felt his clothes and shoulder. He couldn't see or feel a scratch on him. His injuries were completely healed, as though the whole fight had never happened.

"Wow."

"Yeah. Pretty sick, huh? One of the perks of being a Moderator," Kalen replied with a knowing nod and grin. She took his hand and said, "Come on; let's get out of here. I bet our friends are worried. And we're missing an awesome movie."

"You're still ready to watch a movie after all *that*?" Jason cried, still wondering what a Moderator was.

"Yeah," Kalen said with an expression that was blank but with a hint of stern caution. "What of it?"

"Uh, nothing rea— Ugh!" He felt a hand and sharp nails boring into his temples. His head started to pound as though he'd hit pavement. His knees dropped like weights and everything was blurry.

"Forget what you saw. It was a dream," he heard who he thought was Kalen say in a cutting voice.

Jason's world went black.

CHAPTER 3

When Jason came to, he couldn't remember anything. With each staggered step he took out of the bathroom, more and more memories began to surface. Someone, or something, monstrous lunging at him. A glowing rapier. A familiar voice. *"Who sent you, Shadowmonster?"* A threatening one. *"Forget what you saw. It was a dream."*

Jason's whole body was throbbing. What had happened? Had he been mugged? He frantically checked his person for his wallet and found that everything was exactly where it was supposed to be.

As he stumbled out of the bathroom, another memory came to him. Kalen?

What had happened in there?

It was a dream.

For some reason, that was exactly what he felt compelled to believe. It was what his mom always told him anyway. He shook off his confusion and headed back to the movie theater.

Once inside, Jason realized the movie was already halfway done. He walked along the aisles and saw Dimitria looking over her shoulder at him with a furrowed brow. He gave her a sheepish smile and sat down.

He laughed nervously. "Just had a lot of butter to remove, that's all."

"Okay …" Dimitria side-eyed him and grabbed a handful of popcorn. Jason knew that expression meant she wasn't convinced but was trying not to say anything.

When Kalen got back to her seat, Jason's ears perked up. Had he really seen her, or was it just a dream?

"What happened to ya? We were getting worried!" Gage exclaimed way to loudly for a movie theater.

"You were in there a lo-ong time," said Amelia.

"I'm fine, I just had a lot of butter to remove. This is a pretty new top," said Kalen.

Gage impatiently motioned to her seat. "Come on, sit down already. You're missing all the good parts!"

During the rest of the movie, Jason squirmed in his chair, not paying attention to the plot at all. He was drained from passing out in the middle of the bathroom for no apparent reason, and he kept having weird flashbacks about Kalen. More insistently, he needed to know what a "Moderator" was. His eyes darted back and forth over the heads of the people in front of him, while his foot tapped against the carpeted floor.

"What's with you? Are you even watching

the movie?" Dimitria nudged him.

"Yeah, I'm watching. It's nothing," he lied.

*   *   *

When the movie was over, Kalen, Gage, Amelia, and Sandro got up from their seats and headed to the lobby. Amelia and Sandro both needed to use the restroom, so Gage and Kalen had a few minutes to talk.

Gage turned to her and asked in a hushed voice, "What the hell happened in there? You get attacked by a bathroom monster or somethin'?"

Kalen maintained steady eye contact and said nothing for a good minute, making his eyes widen. He tried his best to suppress a laugh. Kalen glared back at him.

"So, it's been taken care of, right? The 'toilet monster'?" He gave Kalen a subtle wink.

Kalen sighed and slumped onto the wall. "Yeah, it's been taken care of. But we have another problem, alright? Jason … from school … the guy that was sitting in front of us that spilled popcorn on me? He saw me."

Gage's expression hardened and he motioned her over to somewhere a little more secluded. "A guy? What do you mean he saw you?"

"The Shadowmonster attacked him and so I rescued him. And he saw me defeat it."

Gage was obviously attempting to conceal how nervous he was, but he wasn't doing a good job of it. "Okay … What did you do about it? You didn't just let him walk out, did you? You know no one's supposed to know about those things. About us. What we do to them."

Just then Amelia and Sandro appeared. Kalen made her face a mask of indifference and hoped Gage was doing the same. Luckily, the two announced that they were heading home and they all said quick goodbyes. Once Amelia and Sandro were safely out of earshot, Kalen started up again.

"I … knocked him out. He woke up, obviously, but he probably thinks he passed out and dreamed the whole thing … right?" Kalen's chest tightened.

Gage groaned and crumpled himself against the wall behind him. "This is not good. This is *so* not good."

"I know! I don't know what to do!"

"Hold on. I have an idea. I saw this in a movie once. So, we sneak up behind him, right? Then—"

"No! We can't hurt him, obviously!"

"Alright, what do you suggest we do, then?" Gage exhaled indignantly.

Kalen darted her eyes, making sure no one could overhear them. That was the last thing they needed. But it was getting late, and the place was emptying out. Then she felt an outstanding jolt course throughout her body.

"Hang on! Did you feel that?" she asked. Dumb question. Gage looked as though he were in just as much shock as her.

"Yeah. I did. Ow! Looks like we got bigger fish to fry."

Kalen nodded. To be honest, she was glad to leave, even if it were to fry bigger fish. The smell of popcorn and spilled slushies was starting to make her nauseous.

*   *   *

After the movie, Jason and Dimitria parted ways and went home. Dimitria had asked if he wanted to grab something to eat before heading home, but Jason declined. His arms and legs were as heavy as cement blocks and he felt a throbbing pain in his back. Try as he might, he couldn't stop thinking about what happened at the movies. On the way to the subway, he noticed Kalen out of the corner of his eye. Who was that guy she was with?

Tall, dark hair, light bluish eyes … Wasn't it the guy from earlier? Before Archery Club?

He remembered the boy making faces at him in the hallway. How jealous he was of his nicer shoes and backpack.

They were whispering back and forth and

walking quickly, as though they were upset about something. What could've happened? Could it be connected to what happened to him in the bathroom? He had to find out.

As he walked up to them, he noticed something odd. On the backs of both of their hands were glowing marks in the shape of a sun.

Aren't they a little young to have tattoos? No, those aren't tattoos. They're glowing.

He hid himself within a group of people ambling down the sidewalk, squinting to inspect the marks further. They looked really familiar. Those weren't just any old glowing sun marks. They were of the symbol of Apollo, the Greek god of light and the Sun.

Were Kalen and her obnoxious friend part of some kind of Apollo-worshipping cult? Nah, they couldn't be. At least not Kalen. She was far too straight laced—a literal straight-A student and an amazing athlete.

Or was that all a diversion to avert suspicion?

*   *   *

Kalen and Gage stood outside the movie theater, their wrists aching from the burning of their marks. They quickly put on their gloves so as not to attract any attention.

"As far as I'm concerned, this is the only good thing about the cold weather here in New York," Gage murmured to Kalen as he pulled his black gloves into place.

They knew there had to be trouble nearby, because that was the only time the marks appeared. So Kalen followed her instincts and headed down to Bryant Park. Every so often there would be some trouble over there, though they didn't yet know why.

"Back to Bryant Park we go, then," Gage whispered to Kalen as they hurriedly turned the corner on 42nd Street.

"What do you mean 'we'? From what I'm sensing, this seems simple enough to be a one-man or one-*woman* job," Kalen snapped.

"Can never be too careful. Why don't I come with you just in case you need backup?"

Kalen let out an exasperated sigh. "For the last time, I've been doing this just as long as you have. You don't need to treat me like a baby. Ugh, fine. Come, but no getting carried away there."

"Whatever do you mean?" Gage smirked.

Kalen took note of his playful smirk before making a face and lightly jabbing on the arm. "I know you! You're just inviting yourself along for fun, aren't you?"

"Maybe …" Gage slyly shifted his eyes in the opposite direction.

"This is exactly why I'm better suited to this job than you," Kalen said, only half joking.

Soon they arrived in Bryant Park, which was surrounded by enormous sets of stairs on each side and welcomed them with a large, open grass field, dim in the evening light.

*   *   *

Jason pursued them into the park, his instincts leading him to follow Kalen and her friend to Bryant Park. The park was always so vibrant and colorful in the fall season. There were better parks, like Central Park, but Bryant Park had its charms. If it were daytime, he could better appreciate it.

From a distance, he watched Kalen and her friend stop to talk as they scanned the area, as though they were predators on the hunt. He'd seen enough of the Discovery Channel to know that they weren't on some pleasant nightly stroll. They were after something. But *what*? He crept closer so he could hear them.

"Okay, Gage. You look this way, I'll look that way," Kalen ordered her friend, who was apparently named Gage.

Jason took another step up the stairs after them, his hand gliding over the railing, but then jerked his hand back, as if he'd been bitten. "Damn static," he grunted, giving his hand a little shake.

Weird, but not the weirdest thing that'd happened to him. He shook it off and kept in pursuit, following Kalen.

When turned a corner, so did he. When she zipped behind a bush, so did he. Soon, Kalen and Gage both reached a section of the park with sets of chess tables. He scanned the area for anything suspicious but saw nothing. But for some reason, Kalen scrunched up her face. He heard her murmur something to her friend. Their hands started glowing again and they exchanged knowing glances.

"Gage! You heard that, right?"

"Yeah."

"I'm gonna go check it out.

Jason heard a rustling in the bushes and panicked. Suddenly, something lunged at him and he screamed. Whatever was on top of him felt heavy and he struggled to wriggle away.

Kalen charged toward the direction of the noise. Gage's hands started to glow and out came a barrage of luminous white bullets.

Without hesitation, Kalen kicked the creature off of Jason.

"Go!" she ordered him with a wave of her hand. She launched herself after the dark monster, aiming her rapier at what she assumed to be the nape of its neck.

Jason nodded, scrambling to his feet and

ducking behind a large ceramic bust that stood on the side of the walkway.

Beneath the streetlamp where it had landed, the creature revealed its long centipede-like body. It shot out of sight, dodging Kalen's strike. Gage fired at it, but its serpentine-like movements dodged his bullets. It lunged at him, sinking its claws into his shoulder, making him grunt and forcing him to hunch down in order to shake it off.

"Gage!" Kalen yelled, sprinting to his side.

Gage managed to grab the creature by its squishy exoskeleton.

"Hang on! Stay outta the way for a sec," he said as the hand he had the centipede creature in started to glow.

Gage looked as though he was beginning to get tired. It was taking a sizable chunk of his energy to make the glowing light in his hand expand and crush the creature. He toppled over into a nearby tree, panting.

Kalen leaned by his side and asked, "Hey, you okay?"

"Welp, that's another one for me. Shit … I'm so drained."

"Yeah, no kidding. You really overextended yourself this time. Be more careful," said Kalen.

"Yeah, yeah, I will, Mom."

Gage sat down in the grass while Kalen bent down and inspected his neck.

"Just making sure that scratch that little guy gave you didn't get you too bad."

"Oh, ha ha," Gage said through gritted teeth.

Jason walked out from behind the pillar and asked, "What the hell was that thing?"

Kalen exchanged glances with Gage, and was about to say something when police sirens began to blare. She turned to Jason, gave him an apologetic frown.

She whipped her head to glare at Gage. "Someone must've heard the gunshots and phoned the police!"

"They're pulling up at the block! Come on, we gotta go!" Gage went up behind them and pushed them behind a bush.

Without hesitation, the three of them broke into a crouching sprint out of the officers' lines of view. Jason moved as fast as his legs could carry him, but he was quickly falling behind. He had no idea about Kalen's agility, or Gage's. He saw her running laps with her other clubmates after school, but it was nothing like this.

He followed them to a flight of stairs, but soon realized he had missed a step as he felt himself colliding onto hard concrete. He jetted back up to see that Kalen and Gage were already far ahead of him. *Great.*

He managed to haul himself out of the park at the very least. Behind him he saw flashes of light followed by tall blue silhouettes. He quickly maneuvered his way past the crowd trying to keep up with the blurring shape of his rescuers. When he got across the street, he leaned onto a building to catch his breath. It was too late.

CHAPTER 4

After about twenty minutes, Gage and Kalen managed to find a cafe that was still open at this hour and sat at the table. The cafe's lighting was dim, lit with small globular light fixtures hanging from the ceiling. There were shadows in every crevice. The room was brown from top to bottom and with a slender island table down the middle. Though it was still open, there were very few people waiting in line and sitting at the tables.

Down to the left, there was a glass case full of delicious pastries, guarded carefully by the cashier, who was eyeing the two suspiciously, probably because they had plopped into a vacant table without having ordered anything.

Gage eyed the pastries by the register, squirming and stretching in his seat. "Man, I'm hungry. I'm gonna go get something from over there." He pointed to the pastries up front, then stood up.

Kalen furrowed her brow. "How? You just got done stuffing your face with junk food at the movies."

"Well, that fight we just got out of brought back my appetite!"

"Whatever, just go," Kalen said, waving him away.

When Gage left, Kalen sat at her seat and stared at the dull brown wall. She thought of the creature at the park. The creature that attacked Jason in the movie theatre. Why were they there? What did they want with Jason?

Jason, she thought. *And we just left him in the park to fend for himself. Jason, who can't know about any of this!*

Moments later, she saw a figure hobble past to the window, and then turn into the cafe and walk over to her. Jason plopped himself into the seat that had been Gage's and looked her dead in the eye.

"What. The. Hell. Guys? You. Left. Me. All. Alone," Jason panted with each breath.

Kalen stammered, "Oh … god ... are you okay?"

"Yeah, now. I just narrowly escaped."

Kalen nodded, quickly trying to figure out how to deal with the situation. She decided to just act normal and come up with a better plan later. "Yeah, sorry about that. So, you gonna get anything? That cashier has been side-eyeing us ever since we sat down."

Jason looked to where Kalen had gestured.

"They don't seem to take too kindly to people lounging in their place of business without buying anything," she whispered loudly.

"I'm actually not feeling food right now. I see your friend up there. Maybe that's enough to stave off the cashier."

He seized the opportunity and asked, "So, what was up with that … creature that attacked us in the park? To be honest, it seemed like you guys were ... tracking it."

Just what Kalen wanted to avoid. She shook her head, "We weren't. We were just taking a walk."

Jason's expression sank a bit. He didn't look convinced. He continued, "So … you and your boyfriend there …?"

Kalen shook her head. "No, no, no. He's not my boyfriend. Gage and I have been friends since middle school! Besides, he has a type, and I'm not it."

Jason was obviously trying to conceal a smile. He caught himself and got back onto the topic at hand. "So … you and your friend Gage were taking a walk when suddenly this creature attacked you? You guys seemed to take the whole thing in stride, seeing as how you whipped weird glowing weapons out of nowhere to defeat it. What's the deal, huh?"

A bead of sweat emerged from Kalen's head. There was a long pause at the table. Jason leaned forward, his patience obviously wearing thin. Then a hand materialized on Jason's shoulder.

"Hey, guys. Everything okay?" Gage's voice

cut through the silence like a dagger.

Jason jumped, "Um, hi. Yeah, just having a quick conversation with Kalen."

Gage continued eying Jason. "Conversation about what?"

As badly as the sight of this tall dark-haired guy talking down his neck obviously made Jason sweat, he got to the point. "Something attacked me at the movies, and then something else attacked us at the park. I want to know why, and what they are. I want to know what you guys are exactly, what that white glowing stuff that comes out of you guys is, and why you're running around fighting those shadowy things."

Okay, so Jason remembered the Shadowmonster from the movie theater.

Gage said in a low voice. "Listen, I think we need to discuss this somewhere a little more private."

"Uh-uh. I almost died, like, *twice*. And I'm pretty sure I remember that glowing stuff coming out of me, too. I need to figure out what's going on *now*." Jason shook his head.

"Coming out of *you* …?" Kalen furrowed her brow. She paused a moment to think back to when she found him in the bathroom of the movie theatre. She thought she had sense something off about the scene. The shadow girl was moving slowly as though she had taken a hit of some kind.

But could it have been from him?

She and Gage exchanged skeptical looks and then she looked back at Jason. "If what you're saying is true, that changes things."

Gage added sternly, "But you had better not be makin' this shit up."

"Well … I'm pretty sure that's what happened. Some things are a little blurry since *someone* knocked me out." Jason shot Kalen a glare.

Kalen looked to Gage nervously, then let out a groan and said, "Fine. We'll tell you whatever you want to know."

Gage shook his head but he seemed resigned to telling Jason. Kalen turned to Jason. "But we need to go somewhere more private. I promise we're not going to ditch you like at the park."

Jason got up and shot her a sideways look. "Or knock me out and run like at the movies?"

"Obviously. So, shall we?"

The three of them got up and left the cafe, Gage uneasily sipping the hot cocoa and scarfing down the last bite of a cream puff he bought as they walked back in the direction of the park.

"Um, back to the park? You sure that's a good idea?" Jason winced.

"Do you want answers or not?" Gage snapped.

Jason nodded. "Proceed," he said, but he

looked like it was the last thing he wanted to do.

*   *   *

Elsewhere in a lush, plant-filled apartment in the Upper East Side with a sign reading Morrigan Manor, Mrs. Morrigan, a stern, red-haired woman with a sleek bob cut, was tapping her foot as she stared out of her living room window.

"Kalen has been gone a long time. I wonder if she ran into some trouble on the way home. I should call and make sure. Maybe she needs backup."

"Oh, Candace, I'm sure she's fine. I keep telling you, your daughter can handle herself. Besides, Gage is with her, too, isn't he?" said a burgundy-haired woman laying on the couch sipping a goblet of a dark red wine.

Mrs. Morrigan put her phone on the glass table near the couch and sat down by her burgundy-haired friend. She plucked the goblet out of her hand and sighed, "You must have a lot of faith in him if you can sip your wine so calmly while he's out dealing with who knows what this late at night."

*   *   *

"Uh, why are we here again?" Jason asked.

"Just be patient, will you?" Kalen snapped.

She unleashed a glowing orb of light and pressed into the palm of Jason's hand.

"Whoa, what's happening? Why is it shaking?" Jason's heart beat out of his chest.

"Just shut up and close your eyes." She was probably trying to be reassuring, but it just came off as cold and bossy.

"Kalen?"

Silence.

"Kalen?"

Still no response.

Jason was falling and he had no idea where to. But at this point he didn't want to know anything anymore. All he wanted was to go home where it was safe. There was a bright light. It grew bigger and bigger the faster he fell towards it. Soon it engulfed him, then darkness did. Suddenly, he felt himself fall hard on the ground.

CHAPTER 5

At first, he heard Kalen's voice. "Jason?"

Then he heard a womanlier voice. "Jason? Are you alright?"

"Yeah …" he managed to say weakly. He was pulled up to his feet by a familiar redhead.

"Sorry. I guess I forgot to tell you what to do before I teleported us here," she said apologetically.

"Kalen, you must be more careful next time. He could have been seriously hurt!" the woman scolded her.

"Right, mother. I won't do it again."

"Mother? Where are we?" Jason turned to Kalen and asked weakly.

"We're at my apartment, Jason. This is my mother."

"Nice to meet you, Mrs. Morrigan," Jason said. He tried to sound polite but it came out a bit awkwardly.

"Hello, Jason. It's a pleasure to meet you, too," she replied, her posture and voice prim and proper.

She had her daughter's red hair but wore it in a razor-sharp bob. She stood straight and firm with her hands at her sides. On one of them, Jason noticed, she wore a bright silver ring in the shape of a crow's skull. Just glancing at it sent chills down his spine.

"W-what are we doing in your house, Kalen?" Jason asked.

"You wanted to know what Moderators are, and now you're going to find out," said Kalen.

"Wait, you teleport this boy here and now this? What is going on here?!" Mrs. Morrigan cried.

Kalen turned to her and said, "Mother, he's one of us. He has Spirit Energy."

Mrs. Morrigan raised her eyebrows in disbelief. "Does he now?"

"Yes, Mother. I saw it myself! I didn't see it for what it was at first, but now I know. He was attacked at the movies … He has the power."

Mrs. Morrigan looked him up and down. He sensed she just saw a scrawny doe-eyed boy.

"If he is what he claims to be, then show me."

"What?" Jason asked.

"Prove it. Prove to me that you're one of us."

"But Mother, he can see them …"

"Kalen, that's enough. Let me handle this," Mrs. Morrigan's voice tightened, commanding the room without having to raise it.

"P-prove? How do I do that?"

"Summon your energy. If you can summon

the power, then you're one of us."

"I … don't know how to do that." Jason rubbed the back of his neck nervously.

"Then I can't help you," said Mrs. Morrigan.

"But I do have something that I think might convince you … It's at home …" Jason continued on with even more hesitation in his voice.

"Is that so?" she replied with a doubtful huff, stroking her chin sternly. "Come back with this proof and maybe then we'll talk."

Jason nodded and began walking slowly toward the front door.

Kalen nodded as well and left the room with Jason. She matched his pace and said reassuringly, "Hey. I know you're legit. My mother on the other hand … Don't take it personal. We need to be very careful about who we let in."

"I can tell … Suddenly I'm not so sure about this … I mean how does the government not know about any of this?"

"Oh, they do," Kalen replied. "They just kind of leave us to our own devices and only get involved when staying out of it is more inconvenient. Listen, come back with whatever it is you said you'd bring, and we'll talk more tomorrow."

"Okay, I'll bring it over then." Jason nodded, pulling his phone out of his pocket. Whoa, that was a lot of angry texts from Dimitria and his mother!

"So, how do you plan on getting home?" asked Kalen.

Jason opened his mouth to answer but then realized he had no idea how he was going to get home. "I don't know actually. I live in Staten Island and have this route I usually take from school, but … what part of Manhattan are we in, exactly?"

"Oh shoot, Staten Island? Wow, that's a trek!" Kalen said with a twinge of guilt in her expression. "So, we're on the Upper East Side. Not too far from Central Park. Come on, at least let me walk you to the closest bus. It's the least I can do."

*   *   *

Gage, Beatrice, and Sandro were hanging out in the park after dropping Amelia off at the bus stop. Gage felt half worried and half rejected.

Gage had texted his friends to see if they wanted to hang out after Kalen teleported off with Jason. He hadn't heard from Kalen since.

He trudged down the street, Beatrice following his lead. She took a seat on a bench and he remained standing, looking up at the moon.

Sandro stood behind him and said, "Full moon … Beautiful, huh? But it's a bad omen. Sinister things are happening as we speak."

Gage squirmed away from him and replied,

"Don't sneak up on me and say shit like that! You know it freaks me out."

"Sorry, man. Can't help it." Sandro chuckled.

Beatrice, who was sitting on the bench, giggled.

"What're you laughing about?" Gage lightly shoved the two of them.

Beatrice stopped giggling but still smiled. The three of them walked down to the subway station and continued chatting on the train platform.

Sandro said, "Don't worry. Wherever she is, I'm sure she is fine. You know she can take care of herself."

"Right." Gage sighed. Sandro was right. He had no real reason to be worried.

"I know you're worried but I'm sure she's fine, too." Beatrice smiled.

"How about a night on the town to take your mind off all this? A trip to the Games and Custard in Times Square? It's All-You-Can-Eat Custard Night!" said Sandro.

"Yeah! It'll be fun, and we'll call them in the morning," said Beatrice.

"Yeah! And when we get tired, you're, as always, welcome to spend the night at our place, Sandro. There's plenty of room!" Gage said.

Gage finally perked up and gave his two friends a wide grin. And with that, the trio hopped onto the next train in search of fun and, more importantly, custard.

*   *   *

On his way to Staten Island, Jason winced as he scrolled through a wall of text messages that were the length of a whole short story from Dimitria and his mom.

Jason where the hell are you?

Jay why aren't you answering my texts? Is everything okay? I'm getting really worried.

His stomach churned with guilt reading them. How could he have let himself get so distracted that he overlooked all of these messages? But then, he'd been running away from monsters and going through portals all evening, and that would make a person a little distracted. But now he had no excuse not to reply.

Sorry Dimi. Something really weird happened. I'll explain tomorrow at school.

As he typed, he wondered if he could explain it to Dimitria at school, or ever. Jason looked out the window as the express bus drove down the Verrazano Bridge and marveled at the bright twinkling city skyline across the water. To think that tomorrow morning, he would be hopping back on the bus again to watch that same skyline going in the opposite direction just like it was any other day.

*   *   *

When Jason got off the bus and onto his front doorstep and reached for the doorknob, the neighbor's dog barked up a storm, waking up his heart rate and the whole neighborhood. The front porch light turned on, the bright light stinging his eyes. The front door opened with a bang and his mother awaited with an angry glower.

"Where the hell have you been? Do you have any idea what time it is?"

"Uh, I got sidetracked …" Jason said, scratching his head nervously.

"*Sidetracked*? It's 2:00 in the morning! I thought you were going to the movies with Dimitria."

"I *was* at the movies, but then something … happened ... and I got stuck up in the city," Jason answered, not meeting his mom's eyes as he went in the door and removed his shoes.

"What happened?" his mom said with a mix a skepticism and concern.

"A … fight broke out at the movie theater and I got separated from Dimitria. I went to a cafe to calm down, but then all the commotion from the movie theater caused a bunch of traffic …" It wasn't a complete lie, Jason figured. A fight *did* break out at the movies. A *supernatural* one, but it sure as hell counted as a fight. He *did* get separated from Dimitria. And yes, there *was* an unusual amount of traffic on the bus ride home.

His mother let out a sigh and motioned him over for a hug. When they embraced, she gave him a tap upside the head and said, "Don't scare me like that again. Call next time if you're going to be running so late!"

"Yes, mom." Jason nodded and hugged back.

When they pulled out of the hug, she motioned him upstairs for bed. He went upstairs and into his room where his faithful black leather notebook was lying on his oak desk right next to his gaming PC. After the crazy night he had, he was too exhausted to think let alone bother with his notebook right now so he washed his face in the bathroom and collapsed in bed.

The next day, Jason slipped the notebook into his backpack and caught the express to school. Even though he'd been attending this prep school for a few months already, when he arrived at the entrance to Whitewood High, he couldn't help but marvel at the prep school's elaborate Gothic stone architecture, with an even four head carvings and the name "Dwayne Whitewood High School" protruding from the columns of the entryway.

On the entrance pathway, he walked among

his classmates, scanning the area for Kalen. When he got to the entrance, however, Dimitria was there, glowering at him.

Jason chuckled nervously and said, "Hey, Dimi. Did you get my text last night?"

"I should be asking you that, jackass! Where were you all night?" she snapped.

He motioned her off to the side. What he couldn't tell her last night was bursting out of him now. "There's something I have to tell you about last night! It was crazy! You know how I've talked to you about seeing strange things growing up that no one else could see?"

Dimitria nodded, squinting her eyes at him.

"When I went to the bathroom to clean myself up, something attacked me," Jason continued on, knowing how crazy this must sound.

"Something? Not someone?" Dimitria asked, her tone shifting from anger to curiosity.

"Something. It was dark and shadowy and … next thing I knew Kalen was there and she rescued me!"

"Huh? Kalen? Went into the boy's bathroom … and rescued you? What do you mean?" Dimitria's eyes began to narrow.

"Well …" Jason started gesturing with his hands, a poor attempt at mimicking Kalen's fencing moves from last night. "I know this sounds crazy, but she fought the thing that was attacking me. A glowing sword came out of her arm … a-and there was a glowing mark on her arm, like a tattoo, but not really …"

"Stop." Dimitria put her palm out in front of him. "You mean to tell me Kalen has some kind of supernatural powers or something?" She crossed her arms. "I knew something was off about that girl! And that guy she hangs out with … *Gabe*?"

"*Gage*. I'm not a fan of him either. He's kind of a prick, but he was there and all glowing too," Jason chimed in. "They both seem to be involved in some kind of secret group that's trying to stop the weird supernatural shit going on around here. And since I can see it too, Kalen tried putting in a good word for me with her mom, who is also part of this thing. But she said she needs proof that I'm like them."

"Jason, I dunno, man. You know I'm here for the supernatural shit, but this sounds kinda weird, like they're trying to recruit you, you know, into a cult," said Dimitria.

"You know, they were giving off weird cult vibes. But, on the other hand, maybe they have the answers I've been looking for all these years. Why I can see the things I see. What it all means and what I can do about it."

"Jason—" Dimitria started, but before she could continue, the school bell rang.

"Crap, Dimi, we gotta get to class."

"Wait, Jason. I don't trust these people. I'm going with you next time in case anything happens."

"I don't know. They seem wary of outsiders."

Dimitria's eyes narrowed. "Outsiders? Jason, do you hear yourself? This all seems …" She shook her head and when she continued, her voice was cold. "You know what? Sure. But if *anything* sketchy goes on, you book it the fuck out of there, got it?"

"Got it." Jason nodded. "See you at lunch later."

"See you at lunch," Dimitria uttered halfheartedly. Guilt made Jason's feet heavy as he ran off to class.

*   *   *

At lunchtime, Jason swam through the sea of hungry prep school students and found Dimitria waving to him from one of the tables on the far right of the Gothic room, by the window. He wound through the room over to her table when he felt someone's arm swoop under his and pull him aside.

"Hey, what's the big id—? Kalen?"

"So, do you have the proof you were talking about?" she asked, pulling him over to the nearest corner. Gage was nowhere around.

"Yeah, I do!" Jason perked up, rummaging through his backpack for his notebook and grinning ear to ear. "Check it out! So, since I was a kid I've been seeing strange people in my house, on my way to school, all kinds of places. People nobody else seems to be able to see. My mom always told me I was just seeing things or feverish or whatever. But I always had the feeling that wasn't the case. And so I've been writing down everything I've seen in this journal. Here. Take a look."

Jason handed the notebook over to Kalen, who scanned it thoroughly before handing it back to him with narrowed eyes and pursed lips. She reminded him of a cat harshly judging the food in its bowl.

"This checks out … You're not messing with me, right?" Kalen asked with a stare so piercing, he was worried he'd get his eye poked out with her rapier if he gave off the wrong vibe.

Jason shook his head, his fingers running over the cover of his notebooks. "N-no! I promise I'm not messing with you. I haven't told anyone about all this stuff." His thoughts turned to Dimitria but he didn't say anything. "I wouldn't just make something like this up."

Kalen's gaze softened and she said, "Okay then. Like I said, I know you have some kind of sense for the supernatural, otherwise you wouldn't have been able to see the Shadowmonsters last night. It's just that my mother, you know, and Gage … I just want to know that you're taking this seriously. This is dangerous work, being a Moderator. The creatures you'd be taking on alongside us could kill you. Understand?"

Kill him? Jason couldn't help but let out a louder gulp than he'd intended to.

"Yes, I understand," he answered. He made his way over to the lunch table where Dimitria was sitting and glaring at him, wondering how much he should tell her.

*   *   *

Earlier that morning, Gage woke up to find himself on the living room floor, the hardwood covered in blankets and potato chips. He had a pounding headache. Beatrice had warned him not to stay up as late as he did. But did he listen? Noooo. He yawned and staggered to his feet. Before he knew it, he was walking—slowly and zombie-like, but walking nonetheless. He turned to see Sandro asleep on the couch. He trudged down the hallway, turned to his left to the bathroom, where he caught Beatrice, who was already dressed, humming to herself and carrying a bundle of towels. He could feel the warmth of the towels from where he stood.

Good old Beatrice.

He walked over to her and said, "What's the

story, Mornin' Glory?"

She jumped and gingerly tucked a tuft of hair behind her ear. "H-hi Gage … Good morning! I didn't see you there!"

"Hey, are you still using the bathroom? I could really use a shower to wake me up after last night's revelry." Gage grinned.

Beatrice said, a bit frantically, "Oh no, I'm done! I-I'm sorry I kept you waiting."

Gage chuckled and, squeezing her so tightly she dropped a towel, said. "Daw! You don't need to apologize; I just got up!"

"O-oh … okay!" She smiled. "Well, come down soon for breakfast."

"Sure thing!" Gage said, helping her pick up the towel then walking into the bathroom. He sometimes wondered if Beatrice had a thing for him, but she wasn't his type, and anyway she was sort of his sister. It'd been a while since he'd met a girl, or boy, he really liked.

Gage closed the door and immediately undressed. He got into the shower and turned on the hot water. The water shot right onto his chest, waking him up and relaxing him simultaneously. He'd never checked to see if Kalen had gotten in touch. He got out of the shower, wrapped himself in a towel, and pulled his phone out of his pants pocket. No one had called or texted since last night. He let out a sigh and got back in the shower, his shaggy wet hair sweeping over his face.

Now I really am worried, Gage thought.

After a few minutes, he got out of the shower, dried himself off on his now-damp towel, and then slipped on his clothes and walked out.

*   *   *

After school, Jason met up with Kalen and they rushed over to the Morrigan home to speak with Mrs. Morrigan. The inside of the apartment looked different in the light of day than it had in the dead of night. It was more inviting and verdant, filled with lush foliage and giving off the vibe of an old Irish castle.

It was like its own world, complete with a crisp, mysterious air. It had a magnetic energy that made Jason never want to leave and gave him the strangest sense of déjà vu. Something coiled in his stomach and for a moment he almost forgot what he'd come here to do.

"Let's get moving," was all Kalen needed to say to break him out of the trance.

Jason followed Kalen into the room where he'd met Mrs. Morrigan the night before. She was sitting in a chair reading what appeared to be a very old book.

"Oh, you again? So, you've come back with proof of your affinity for the supernatural?" she asked sharply.

He walked slowly over to her and left his notebook on the table next to her.

"What's this?" she asked as she got up from her seat with the notebook in her hand.

"It's a journal I keep … of all of the supernatural things I've seen over the years." Suddenly, he wondered why he'd brought his notebook at all and what kind of proof it offered.

"A journal, you say? Let's see what's in it, then." She opened up the notebook and read it. Jason caught Kalen eyeing her mother, looking more on edge than she usually did.

Mrs. Morrigan was difficult if not impossible to read as she devoured the pages of Jason's notebook. When she was finished reading it, she handed it back to him and said, "This is quite the grimoire of ghosts you've got logged in here. I've heard of most of these, but there are some entries in here that I knew nothing about. You do have a sense for the supernatural, it would seem."

Jason beamed. Someone finally believed him. No, not just believed him, but could see the same things he did.

"But are you a Moderator?" Mrs. Morrigan asked. "I've seen no evidence that you have Spirit Energy, so that is still to be determined. Jason, Kalen, come with me. We're going to figure out for sure what you're capable of in the Chamber of

Energy."

What if I don't want to be a Moderator?
Jason thought, fighting the urge to say out loud.

CHAPTER 6

"**C**hamber of Energy?" Jason repeated, following them.

They walked down a long, winding hallway. It seemed like it stretched on for miles. Further down the hallway, the walls grew narrower and were covered with faded pictures of dead relatives. Then, Mrs. Morrigan turned to a bookshelf and took out one of the books. In the spot where the book had been, there was a stone with a strange carving on it. It glowed when she touched it.

"The old secret passageway behind the bookcase, huh? That's a little cliché!"

"I know, right? I've been telling her to consider redecorating, but ..." Kalen shrugged.

"It's cliché but *effective!*" Mrs. Morrigan snapped back.

The whole bookshelf sunk down into an opening in the floor, revealing a dark path ahead. Cobwebs filled the corners and lights flickered in the distance, revealing a staircase in back.

More dark places? Jason thought. "Uh ... you know what? I change my mind ... I think I'm going to go home ...," he stammered,

"Oh, quit being a baby!" Kalen dragged

Jason by the arm through the dark hallway. He let her pull him forward.

A pair of lit candles were hanging on the sides of the hallway. Mrs. Morrigan grabbed one and kept walking. Kalen picked up the other one and pulled Jason down the stairs with her. The stairs spiraled around, making Jason dizzy. As they walked deeper and deeper down, the path became darker and darker. Thank god for the candles Kalen and her mother were carrying.

Jason awkwardly navigated his feet down the steps, one hand against the cold stone wall. "What is the Chamber of Energy, anyway?"

"It's one of the chambers that we use to recharge our Spirit Energy," Kalen said. "Oh, Spirit Energy is that white, glowing energy that came out of our hands back at the movies. You could do almost anything you want with Spirit Energy … with the right training …"

Jason jumped back at her words. "Wait, what? *Training*?!"

"Well, now you know you have the power, so it would make sense to strengthen it and work on it." Kalen shrugged her shoulders nonchalantly.

"Wait a minute! I don't … I don't even really know what's going on, let alone what I'd be training for!"

"Allow me to better explain," said Mrs. Morrigan, stopping in front of an old door. "There is a secret society, branching worldwide, specializing in interaction with and protection from the supernatural, called the Moderator Society. You, Jason, may soon be inducted into it."

"*Me*?" Jason asked in disbelief.

"We're running short on people since the Outbreak. We're taking all the help we can get," said Kalen.

"Whoa! I never agreed—"

"And we didn't ask," Mrs. Morrigan said, opening the door to a small room. He wasn't sure if she meant that they didn't need to ask him or they might not.

Jason merely looked at her with glazed eyes. After a minute, he asked, "Um, what exactly are we going to do in here?"

"This room is full of Spirit Energy. What we are doing here is revitalizing yours. It seems you were born with these abilities, but for some reason, your powers have only just awakened. So, before you begin training, if you begin training, you need to look within you to activate it," said Mrs. Morrigan.

"O-okay," Jason said timidly, but seriously. He didn't have to join them if he didn't want to, but he wanted to know if he had it. To think, he might have been pulsing with Spirit Energy all these years. "What is the outbreak you mentioned earlier?"

"The Outbreak was the start of a global surge of Shadowmonsters into the world of the living. The first one happened around the time of the zenith of Ancient Greece. It is said that it was the Greek god of light, Apollo, who found a way to fend them off. Since then, other Outbreaks have occurred. From then on, Apollo passed down this power, which we now call Spirit Energy, to a select few in each part of the world, to ensure global protection, of course. That is how the Moderator Society began," Mrs. Morrigan explained.

"The most recent Outbreak happened about eleven years ago. The casualties were massive. The Shadowmonsters almost destroyed the Chamber of Energy, which would have been a nightmare," Kalen said.

A chill went through Jason. How close had the world been to destruction, and he'd never heard anything about it? "Th-that's horrible … I didn't have any idea that was going on … How come the outbreaks of these monsters haven't ever been addressed, or reported on the news or anything, for all of this time? How come the government or the FBI or whatever aren't helping out with all this?"

"Seriously? Because they are supernatural creatures, so only *we*, the Moderators, can see and interact with them. The government does know about us, but they mostly let us fight the Shadowmonsters on our own. The origin of the monsters is unknown, but the Society has been doing extensive research." Kalen continued. "Moderators are like spiritual mediums … but taken up a notch. We take on all kinds of tasks, like mediating with troubled spirits who can't be put to rest for some reason or engaging in combat with Shadowmonsters. We can peacefully resolve the problems of earth-bound souls or fight tainted spirits. That's where Spirit Energy is used. Spirit Energy is our power source."

"I know that much; you told me that already." Jason replied matter-of-factly, making Kalen scowl.

Mrs. Morrigan said, "There have been some revelations as to their origins. It would seem that they have that same dark energy that has corrupted these creatures. There has to be some sort of relation between the two."

"Huh ... makes sense," said Jason.

"Good then. Now step into the circle right over there in the center." Mrs. Morrigan pointed to the center of the room with a large circle of tiles in many different shades of green.

Jason walked to the middle of the circle. When he stepped onto the small round tile at the very center, it began to glow.

"That's it. That's all the confirmation I need. You are indeed one of us. Now, Jason, you must search within you to reawaken your Spirit Energy."

"I … I don't know … From what you've been telling me, this seems like really dangerous work … Maybe you ought to find somebody else. Someone who really knows what they're doing." Why did they want him so bad anyway? Jason remembered what Dimitria had said about them trying to recruit him for some kind of cult and suddenly wished he could be anywhere but that room.

"It is. We'd only be lying if we said it wasn't difficult …," said Kalen. "We thought about asking for help from members from other parts of the world, but they've also got their hands full."

"I understand your hesitation, Jason. However, having you to aid our cause would be most helpful to us. I'm sure being alongside Kalen these past few days has shown you the horrors these Shadowmonsters can inflict on humanity and give you the motivation you need to be convinced," said Mrs. Morrigan.

She was right. As much as he wanted to be anywhere but here, there was nowhere safe to go. He'd been seeing supernatural beings his entire life, and now these Shadowmonsters were attacking him. Jason inhaled deeply, then focused his thoughts on activating the Spirit Energy inside him. He grunted as he tried to bring forth the power.

Mrs. Morrigan said to him, "Focus. Focus on the power surging through you."

Focus, Jason, focus!

Just focus on the Spirit Energy and let it come out of you!

He was, after several minutes, able to feel a small pulse of energy flowing to his hands. "Alright! I did it!" he cried. "This is cool! I did it!"

"Awesome! Just a bit more!" Kalen urged.

But the vibration of energy in Jason's hands started to wane. He opened his eyes and looked from Kalen to Mrs. Morrigan and back again.

Jason closed his eyes again and grunted and groaned for about ten minutes until he was panting in exhaustion.

Kalen sighed exasperatedly and barked, "Come on! I've seen more hustle in a game of chess! Push harder!"

Jason, now embarrassed and intimidated, took a deep breath, found his center, and began again. This time he pushed for almost twenty minutes, the energy getting a bit stronger, but then disappearing quickly, to his chagrin.

Kalen groaned and turned to her mother. "We have to find a way to get his Spirit Energy activated."

"Maybe we should trigger the emotions he felt during his first activation," Mrs. Morrigan suggested.

"Yeah. Let's let him know about how—" Kalen started to say.

Her mother interrupted her. "No. We won't tell him. It has to be genuine in order for him to learn. For that he would have to see—"

"You don't mean …?" Kalen shuddered.

"Yes. I do. It's the only way. Corner a wounded dog and it will attack," said Mrs. Morrigan. Jason was too tired to follow their conversation.

"Jason. What do you say about getting some … tutoring?" Kalen chuckled nervously.

"Tutoring?" Jason tilted his head. "There's *tutoring* for this kind of stuff?"

"Yeah … How about first thing tomorrow morning?" Kalen replied, attempting to sound sweet but only sounding awkward.

"I don't know …," said Jason. But he wasn't sure he had a choice.

*   *   *

Jason walked down the hallway from the guest bedroom he had slept in. This time around, he'd called his mother ahead of time to tell her he was staying at a friend's house. He *didn't* tell her that this friend was a girl, a girl he had a huge crush on; she would go insane over the idea of it.

Mrs. Morrigan had been the one to invite him to stay, being that "it was late" and he "was such a long way from home." Kalen blushed profusely at the thought of this. He could tell she'd been reluctant at first, and then shyly went along with it. He'd more or less felt the same way with a smidge of "hell yeah" thrown in there.

So, here he was, waking up from spending the night in his crush's swanky apartment on the Upper East Side. As he strode down the corridor, he saw rows of portraits on the walls. The people in the portraits all looked very similar. When he first saw of their hair, he was reminded of all of the colors of autumn, from bright red to strawberry blonde to a dull reddish brown. The next thing he noticed was that they all had bright emerald green eyes, and each of them donned that intense stare that Jason knew all too well. He read the names of people in the portraits.

Abiageal, Adan, Annabelle, Christina, Fianna, Fiona, Morgan Morrigan ...

Aegis, Medea, Agatha, Iris, Samantha, Patricia ...

Sabrina, Ferris, Alice Morrigan, Candace, Nora Morrigan ...

With a flash of surprise, Jason noticed another similarity the people in all these photos shared. They were all women! He had seen walls like this before. It was like those really wealthy families who only displayed portraits of the patriarchs of the family line, but with women.

Bump!

It was Kalen, who was carrying a plate of pancakes, covered in syrup and strawberries. Luckily, no food was injured in the collision.

"What are you doing holding a plate of pancakes?" Jason asked curiously.

"My mom asked me to bring them up to your room in case you were hungry," Kalen stuttered. Then she said sharply, pushing the plate at him, "Well, you can't train on an empty stomach. Hurry up and eat them so we can go and train."

"Uh, right!" Jason said.

He grabbed the plate of pancakes from her, and then took them downstairs to eat at the table he'd seen in the kitchen. Kalen disappeared somewhere else in the house. "That was awfully nice of her," Jason said under his breath, so as not to run the risk of getting yelled at. Why anyone would yell at him for complimenting them, he had no idea. But it seemed like something Kalen would do.

*   *   *

Some hours later, Jason and Kalen were at the bus stop when an express bus pulled up. Kalen frowned. "You're sure this is the right one, right? The park is on the way to Staten Island," she said.

"Of course! I only take this bus to school and back, like, every weekday!" Jason replied.

"I can't believe you live all the way down in *Staten Island.*"

"Why?"

Kalen paused for a moment, and then mumbled, "Well, I guess transferring to a private school in Manhattan couldn't have exactly been a cheap venture …"

"Huh? Hey, wait a minute! What's that supposed to mean?!" Jason said indignantly.

The two hopped on the bus, waddled past blue eighties-themed aisles, and sat near the front. The minute they sat down, Kalen giggled and said, "I want a full outfit in this fabric." Jason couldn't help but laugh.

He could feel Kalen looking at him—and was that a sweet smile on her face?—as he looked out the window. When he turned his gaze ever so slightly towards her, she looked sharply away. Then she looked back at him when he looked away, and smiled again.

This back and forth continued for almost a half hour until Jason broke the silence. "I never expected such a sweet smile from such a ferocious fencer."

"Huh?" Kalen shook her head and made an abrupt turn in her seat. "You've talked to the other fencers about me? Heard some of the rumors?"

"Well, I might've overheard a few things. Like how you have a hotheaded streak …"

"Ugh. Of course. 'Too hotheaded,' they whine. Weak, pathetic cowards, the lot of them!"

"How you've put people in the hospital …" Jason squirmed in his seat.

Kalen groaned and pressed her thumb and finger to the bridge of her nose. "It wasn't my fault! I told the coaches over and over that it was an accident! They wanted me to prove my worth, so they threw me up against some whelp of a guy, hardly old enough to grow his first chin hairs. I guess they thought a petite girl like me wouldn't be strong enough to hurt a tall guy like him. I didn't mean to get him sent to the hospital! Why would I want that? I just ... lost control."

An awkward silence filled the air for a while.

Jason took out his iPhone from his pocket. He needed to diffuse the tension somehow. He put one ear bud into one of his ears, and then offered the other one to Kalen.

"Wanna listen?" he asked.

"Sure."

She put the ear bud on and listened. It was an upbeat rock song Jason loved. She hummed to the tune sweetly, which Jason found cute.

He chuckled a little and asked, "You've heard this song before?"

"Yeah," she replied.

They both hummed to the song until it was finished, then it changed to another song. This song was more smooth, calm, and romantic.

Maybe it was the song that was doing it, or maybe it was the rocking motion on the bus, but something was making Kalen very sleepy. Her eyelids fell a few times, but she quickly opened them. In the end, her fight was futile and her head rested ever so comfortably on Jason's shoulder. Jason looked at his shoulder, surprised, and pulled her body a little closer to his so she could sleep more comfortably.

She looks so peaceful when she's asleep, like she's in some sort of paradise in her dreams, Jason thought.

About a half hour later, Jason saw that they had reached their destination and woke up Kalen to get off. Kalen opened her eyes and turned bright red. Maybe it was the drool hanging from her mouth, but Jason didn't care about that. Everything about Kalen was cute.

They hopped off the bus and walked to a small park. Jason stretched his arms and said, "Let's *do* this! Where's that tutor?"

"We have to go through the hidden passage," said Kalen.

Jason, not listening, ran into the middle of the field and started jumping, kicking, and shadowboxing. "I'm ready to go! Where's that teacher?" he shouted eagerly.

"Jason, look out!" Kalen shouted from afar, seeming distressed.

"Huh?" Jason lifted his leg up and accidentally kicked something.

He turned to look at his foot and saw a pair of horse's hooves.

"Oh, god! Are you okay?" he cried.

"You need to be more careful! You could've seriously hurt him!" Kalen snapped at Jason.

The owner of the horse hooves trotted closer to him and said in a deep, masculine voice, "Yes, you should—"

Jason recoiled in fear and scampered away from the ferocious being.

"Teacher?" Jason yelped in shock. "That … that *centaur* is our *teacher*?"

"Yeah," Kalen answered, punctuating with a nod of her head. "Shadowmonsters aren't the only creatures we interact with on the regular. As you can clearly see."

Jason turned around and gave her a dubious look. "So they're real? The Greek myths … are *real*?"

Kalen gave him a confused look back. "Yeah, of course they're real. Every fairytale, folktale, spooky ghost story your best friend might've told you as a kid, urban legend you've heard. They're *all* real."

But he already knew that. He just never believed it. Upon hearing confirmation once again that, no, he in fact *hadn't* just been "seeing things" his whole life, Jason felt like the air around him had been sucked away and all that was left was his own reserves of oxygen. When he collected himself, he realized that Kalen wasn't even been looking in his direction anymore and was instead motioning apologetically in the centaur's direction.

"Um, sorry about that, teacher. He's new, *really* new, so he doesn't know what he's doing *at all*." Kalen bowed her head apologetically.

"Ah, I see." said the centaur, "Let's get started, then." He walked to the center of the baseball field and stood quietly.

"What's he doing?" Jason asked Kalen.

She jumped in surprise, apparently unaware of the fact that he had been standing behind her the whole time.

"He's using his Spirit Energy to create a portal that will transport us to the training area, like how I did to teleport us to my house the night before last. Using Spirit Energy to teleport is one of the basics of being a Moderator. You're going to have to learn how to do that at some point," she replied crossly.

"Yeah, I guess." Jason chuckled nervously.

The centaur's hands glowed with Spirit Energy until the energy shot out of his hands and into the sky. It enveloped them and their surroundings and they were blinded by white. Jason looked around nervously, panicking because he couldn't see a thing. He felt a hand latch onto his.

He then heard Kalen say, "Hang on and follow me, or you'll end up like you did last time!"

Jason gripped her hand tightly and let the rushing of the wind blow a mighty gust at him as he felt himself moving away from the ground he stood on.

*   *   *

Gage stood on his parents' apartment rooftop, gazing at the view of all of the buildings in the city. He was so down that he was dressed in just a baggy gray jacket and some jeans he'd found lying around in his room. He was chewing some bubblegum and blowing a bubble. The spring breeze, which made his shaggy hair brush against his face, suddenly popped his bubble. Startled, he opened his mouth and the gum dropped out. He sighed as he watched the gum fall from the twelve-story apartment building.

Damn it! That was my last one. I just don't have any luck lately?

He pulled his cell phone out of his pocket, and then immediately put it right back. He didn't want to think about it right now. He didn't want to think about how one of his best friends abandoned him.

That's the thing about being a foster kid.

You worry whether the new people in your life are just going to disappear forever, like the others before them. Talk is cheap so you analyze every word and every action. It becomes hard to just trust that things will work out.

Suddenly, he heard a loud blast of wind coming from the west. He looked to his left, and there he saw a large, bird-shaped explosion of whiteness. The impact of the blast threw him off balance and he almost fell off the edge of the roof. Instead, he fell backwards with a loud thud.

"Ow! What the hell was that?" he muttered to himself, getting up to standing.

He heard footsteps behind him. It was Beatrice, carrying some sandwiches and water, thoughtful as ever.

"I-I thought you might be hungry," she said to him, smiling.

"Thanks, Trix."

She looked at him seriously and asked, "Are you going to be okay?"

Silence.

"I know you're worried but …"

"I know, I know. She's strong; she can take care of herself. But it's late afternoon and she still hasn't called." said Gage.

Beatrice walked over to him and gave him a reassuring hug. The warmth and comfort of her embrace lit him up.

"I'm sure she'll be fine," Beatrice chirped.

"I hope you're right," Gage turned his gaze back to the horizon ahead, noticing the sun beginning to set.

*   *   *

Jason and Kalen landed in a park similar to the one they were just standing in. Only here, the sky was grey and cloudy, as though it had just rained. The trees surrounding the field were dead, and the park was barren. Shivers ran down Jason's spine.

In a booming voice, the centaur said, "Welcome to the training grounds."

"Why here? It's a little creepy, isn't it?" Jason could hear his own voice quivering.

"Everyone trains here, so you're going to have to deal with it," he replied, his eyebrows knotted.

The centaur then turned to Kalen and gasped with delight. "Now that we have a little privacy, I can greet you properly. Well, hello, Kalen! It's been a long time!" he said.

Kalen chuckled nervously.

"How has my favorite student been doing lately?"

"Just fine, teacher," Kalen said formally.

"Nonsense! You're very welcome to call me

Chiron!" The improbably large, muscular centaur smiled.

Jason perked up at hearing his name, having heard it before in the books he'd read about Greek mythology.

"Where should we begin our lessons? What have you already mastered?" He motioned to Jason.

Jason looked at him without quite meeting his gaze and said, "Well, sir, I'm having a bit of trouble activating my Spirit Energy."

"Wait, you don't even know how to *activate* it?" Chiron chuckled. "Every warrior knows how to do that! It's the most basic of the basics! You need it to summon your weapon!"

Jason looked down in chagrin and muttered, "Yeah. I know. I figured that part out."

Jason stared at the dry brown grass at his feet. What kind of Moderator *was* he? He couldn't even activate his Spirit Energy, a basic! He felt so pathetic in front of this powerful mythological being.

Chiron put his hands to his hips and scanned Jason for a moment or so, with his thumb and index finger cupping his chin, humming and hawing. He cracked his knuckles and then said in a low, strong voice, "Let's get down to business, then. You've got a lot to learn."

Here was his chance! Jason stood up straight and said, "Yeah!"

"*Yes*, what?" Chiron said sternly, clasping his hand to his ear.

"Yes, *teacher* …," Jason replied.

"Good. Now focus on summoning your Spirit Energy," said Chiron.

He focused on his Spirit Energy, closed his eyes, and got to work summoning. Then he felt a painful force pushing against his face. The teacher did a high-jump kick to his face, his strong, heavy hooves nearly crushing his face with the force of a ten-ton brick. He went flying to the other side of the field. He landed face-first on the dirt, staggering to his feet. It was strange he could get up at all. That kick would've incapacitated a trained fighter, let alone a teen boy as scrawny as him.

It must be the Spirit Energy, he assumed. *It must be making me physically stronger and tougher than normal.*

When he managed to be able to collect himself, he wiped some blood off his lip and asked, "What the big idea?!"

"You have to pay close attention in a fight!" said Chiron haughtily. "Never let your guard down!"

"He's right, Jason! Stay sharp!" said Kalen from the bleachers that surrounded the barren field.

"You're just going to sit and watch from the sidelines? I thought you were going help me too!" Jason cried.

"Uh, no. *He's* going to help you. That *is* his job." Kalen replied, as though it were obvious.

"Gee, thanks—" Jason pouted. "Oof!"

He was kicked upside the head again.

"Hey! I wasn't ready! Oof!"

Kicked again.

"Will you quit—? OOF! AUGH!"

Kicked twice. In the *ass*.

Now Jason was getting irritated. "Okay, that's it! Now the gloves are coming off!" he shouted.

He dodged the next kick, then quickly charged the Spirit Energy to his hands and began to strike at the robust centaur attacking him.

The impact of the energy colliding with Chiron's arms sent him flying backward. His hooves slid harshly through the grass, though this did not faze him. He found his footing and smirked.

"Well, well, well. Impressive! So, you *do* have some control over it. Just not enough," he said.

Corner a wounded dog and it will bite back, Jason thought.

"Alright, I was hoping I wouldn't have to do this but you leave me no other choice." Chiron sighed.

"Do *what*?" Jason asked. Before he could ask, Chiron summoned a giant club made of Spirit Energy and swung it at him at full force.

Jason staggered back, the adrenaline kicking

in and screwing with his balance.

"Centuries of training gods, demigods, and Moderators taught me that. Defeat me, and today's lesson is over. That is, if you do not *die*!" Chiron smirked.

"What? Are you crazy?" Jason cried.

He fell but got back up quickly. Panting, he looked up at the sky. Suddenly, a large shadow eclipsed the sun. It was heading straight towards him. A white-hot beam of Spirit Energy. The impact blew him into a tree on the other side of the park. He crashed with a loud *thud*! Then he felt something hit him in the stomach. Hard. It smelled like tree bark and tasted like dirt. His head was hurting, his bleeding lip tasted like rust, and his limbs felt limp as spaghetti as he struggled to get up.

Kalen watched from a set of bleachers set that stood on one side of the field. She stood up. "Jason!" she screamed, "Jason! I'm co—!"

"No! He has to learn for himself. *Corner a wounded dog and it will bite back*," said Chiron.

As Jason was struggling to get up, Chiron said, "How do you feel, boy?"

"How do I *feel*? I feel like I'm going to get killed here! Come on, knock it off! I don't want to *die*!" Jason screamed.

Suddenly, his Spirit Energy started to pulse and his hands began to glimmer.

"What was that?" Chiron said, cupping his hand to his ear.

His eyes widened; he got it. He knew what to do this time. "I don't want to *die* here!" he repeated, with more fury and vigor than the last time. Then his hands started to glow again, and his energy took the form of a bow and arrow.

Jason stepped back. He gingerly maintained a firm stance with the bow in one hand and the arrow in the other hand. He saw Chiron charging at him and didn't hesitate to fire a flurry of arrows at him, making him stumble.

Ha ha! I did it! But can I do it again?" he thought to himself.

"He did it!" Kalen cheered, now standing next to Chiron. "*That* was what he needed to get going. That is the feeling that every Moderator needs to have in order to battle: the fight or flight survival instinct, the need to fight for their life without hesitation."

Jason turned to Kalen and Chiron and gave them a steady thumbs-up before flopping to the ground.

Chiron and Kalen scrambled over to help him up. "Thank god you're safe! Great work, Jason," said Kalen, who put her arm around him protectively.

"Thanks," said Jason, "Why do I have this feeling of déjà vu?"

Kalen looked startled and blushed for a moment, and then said, "Come on. Let's go back. Now that you've got it down, it's time to write you in as a member of the Society."

"Oh, right," Jason said halfheartedly. He was good with training but still unsure about actually becoming a Moderator. "I almost forgot about that."

"Wait a moment, boy! I would like to ask you something!" said Chiron.

"Of course, teacher. What is it?" said Jason.

"Your name is … Jason … if I heard correctly?"

"Yes. Why do you ask, Mr. Chiron?" Jason tilted his head curiously.

"Ah, now it makes sense why fate brought you here to me. You see, I once had a student of the same name as yours." Chiron beamed.

"R-really? I think I've read about him before, but the repeated blows to the head are kind of botching up my memory at the moment. Ha ha." Jason chuckled bashfully.

"Jason, I believe great things are in store for you. Take care."

As Jason and Kalen walked back to the bus stop to return to the Chamber of Energy for his initiation, Jason said to Kalen, "Wow. I was trained by the same person as a legendary hero of Greek mythology! Who knows? Maybe—"

"Yeah, yeah. Don't let it get to your head. Like he mentioned earlier, you've only mastered the *basics*." But something in Kalen's expression told him she was a little impressed by (if a bit jealous of) how he took to his training.

"Geez, way to kill the moment," Jason replied, punching her softly on the arm.

*   *   *

The Chamber of Energy was as dark as ever. Jason and Kalen stepped down the very last step before walking into the dim, candlelit room. Mrs. Morrigan was already there, waiting with that same stoic, proper air.

"So, you're back." She gave him a small smile.

"Yeah, I got it down!" Jason replied impudently.

"Yeah, yeah, yeah. Take it down a notch, Mr. Hero. You still need more training," Kalen said coldly.

Jason looked at her incredulously. Back at the training grounds, she seemed just as happy about it as he was.

"That's right. And you still need to be initiated into the Society. Just step into the center of the circle and call forth your weapon."

"You know, I'm still not completely sure I

want to do this …"

"Well, you were already born with the power, so technically, you're *already* a Moderator. This is just a formality."

"Well, if that's how it works, then here goes nothing," Jason said, walking to the center of the room. To tell the truth, he already felt like a Moderator.

Jason took a deep breath and called up the intense fear, the feeling of being in mortal danger, that he felt training with Chiron and channeled it into his Energy. His bow and arrow took shape, and the tiles on the floor began to glow. A giant ball of purple light emanated from the floor, and when he looked at his arms, he saw black lines spreading up them. He wondered if it was too late to stop the initiation. Then, the black lines grew longer and enveloped his whole arm like a long glove. He uttered a small gasp when it turned into a black circle with a dot in the middle on the back of his hand.

"Don't worry," said Mrs. Morrigan. "The glowing symbol on the back of your hand is a mark that all Moderators have. It only appears when you use your powers, so you won't have to worry about covering it up or anything outside of battle. You are now an official Moderator."

"Wait, that's it? So now I get to go kick some ghost butt?" Jason asked cheerily.

"Well—" Kalen started to say before her body jerked and she let out a groan.

"What's the matter, Ka—? AGH!" Jason said and groaned too.

A wave of adrenaline rushed through his body as an ominous presence seemed to hover over him. The feeling was strange to him. "K-Kalen … what was *that*? It felt so weird."

Kalen had also recovered. "That was the essence of a Shadowmonster. We're able to sense them when they show up and cause trouble," she said. "Looks like you get your chance to 'kick some ghost butt' after all."

"Sweet!" Jason pumped his fist in the air.

"Don't be hasty. You're still inexperienced. At least charge your Spirit Energy before you go," said Mrs. Morrigan.

"Uh, okay. How do I do that?" Jason asked.

"Stay in that circle, then take a deep breath and imagine your energy filling you. Imagine that you're breathing the energy inside you," Kalen instructed him.

She turned to her mother and said quietly, "I think it helps him when he has some kind of imagery in his head. Then he channels it into his powers."

"I see."

Jason did as instructed.

As he took his breath, he felt himself

floating and the energy coursing into him smoothly and effortlessly. It felt almost relaxing, like the cold blowing of the wind. He felt as though he was floating in a pure light, then the light died and he flittered back down. Jason stretched his arms out in front of him and said, "Wow! That felt amazing!"

"Not surprising. Spirit Energy is like regular energy. You use it up through activity, in this case using your weapon. You can have access to more energy by increasing your stamina through experience, or in your case, *training*," Kalen explained.

"So basically, it works the same way as chakra. That makes a little more sense." Jason lit up in understanding.

Now Kalen and her mother were the ones who didn't understand what he was talking about.

"From *Naruto*? *That's* why you guys are so insistent that I train first." Jason chuckled nervously.

Kalen nodded her head in understanding. "Yeah, like that. Gage and I have binge-watched many a Naruto episode at Amelia's house."

"The weapon each Moderator has is formed from their unique energy. Each weapon is shaped by one's instincts, or one's typical way of dealing with conflict, your fight or flight instinct, to put it simply," said Mrs. Morrigan.

"That would explain why my weapon is

different from Kalen's. My weapon is a bow and arrow because I know how to use a bow and arrow, right? That's not so complicated to me." Jason said with a hint of a smile.

"Or maybe because you're the type of person who prefers to avoid direct conflict," Kalen replied bluntly. "For instance, not only am I talented with swords, but I take to all conflict the same way I take my fencing: as quickly but strategically as possible. Though, there are even *more* passive members of the Society called Healers …"

Kalen spent a good moment giving Jason a patronizing stare. "I'm sure it's obvious what *they* do …"

He didn't know if she was insinuating something, but he wanted to go and help out Kalen—and not look like a wimp in front of her. "I want to go fight," he said steadfastly.

"Okay, then. Just watch your back and don't do anything reckless; I can take care of myself," said Kalen.

"Boy, are you going to be in for a surprise," she said under her breath. Then, louder, "The Shadowmonster's presence is somewhere in Staten Island. If you use your Sense, you can probably track it and teleport closer by."

"You're right. Weird. I can see an abandoned house," said Jason.

And with that they teleported back to Staten

Island.

*   *   *

Beatrice walked into the hallway carrying some trays when Mrs. Samson walked by her.

"Oh hello, Beatrice," Mrs. Samson said, smiling.

Beatrice always felt extra nervous around her but still tried to be friendly. "H-hello, Mrs. Samson."

Mrs. Samson let out a slightly exasperated sigh. "Honey, how many times have I told you that you don't have to be so formal! Around here, it's *Jessica*!"

She had a bold presence, a presence so true to the expression "fiery redhead" that she intimidated Beatrice. Everything about the woman's appearance, from her wine-colored hair to her piercing blue eyes to her bright red lipstick, read "eclectic." This was the kind of woman who didn't care what anyone thought.

"I have to go to a meeting. You'll order dinner for us, won't you?" she asked.

"You bet!" Beatrice smiled.

"Good girl!" Jessica pinched Beatrice's cheeks and left.

Beatrice headed on to the kitchen when she stumbled upon something that made her stop in her tracks. Gage was sleeping on the floor of the hallway. He got up, stretching his arms and legs widely. When he got to his feet, he noticed Beatrice standing next to him.

"Um, Gage? Were you napping in the hallway again? You really shouldn't do that; it's bad for your back *and* your sleep patterns," she told him quietly.

"He he, I know. I sat down here to think and then I just dozed off. I guess I didn't have anything better to do." Gage let out a deep sigh.

Beatrice could sense some agitation in him. She had to try to think of a way to keep his mind occupied for a while. "Hey, Gage?"

Gage looked up. "What is it, Trix?"

"M-maybe we can hang out at Midtown Manhattan. You know, we haven't gone there in a while," said Beatrice.

Gage let out a hearty laugh. Beatrice looked at him, a bit confused. Gage said, "*There's* something I never thought I'd hear in my *life*! Before I was adopted into this family, I always wanted to be able to walk all over Manhattan whenever I felt like it. Now I can." He let out an excited laugh and put his hand on her shoulder.

Beatrice smiled and said, "That makes two of us, then."

Then the two of them looked each other in the eyes a moment, smiling at each other. When it sunk in that they had both been staring at each other, they quickly turned away. Beatrice's cheeks felt hot.

Gage said, "Sorry, I just sorta zoned out. Well, what are we just standing around for? Let's go!" Gage dashed to the stairs.

Beatrice ran to catch up with him when Gage suddenly stopped. "Gage, what's wrong? Why'd you stop?" she asked curiously.

Suddenly, she heard the sound of breaking glass, and then she was being held down to the ground by Gage, who had something white in his hand. When she looked up a dark blur shot down from the ceiling and landed near them.

Before she could see what it was, Gage jumped to his feet and pulled her up. Holding her close to him with his left arm, he fired at the creature with his right. When she broke away from him, she realized he was carrying two black-and-white twin pistols in his hands. They were his Moderator weapons, which he affectionately called his "Spirit Fingers."

She saw the serious look on Gage's face and realized they were in mortal danger.

His mouth was inches from her face. "Stay close. This is gonna get dangerous …"

Beatrice quickly agreed. She then let out a startled gasp as a small black figure went straight for her.

Gage's right arm swung in front of her. He held up his handguns, bullets firing rapidly at the horrific looking figure that she could now see more clearly. It landed on the ground and Gage stopped shooting. A giant cleaver was fused to its arm, half of its left leg was nothing but black, rotten bone, and its head was also black and rotted. It got back up and growled at them.

Gage kept his handguns right in front of him and charged at the abomination as it charged at him. "Wanna go, ugly? LET'S GO!"

CHAPTER 7

"**O**w," Jason complained, cradling his head.

"Oh, stop being such a baby!" Kalen told him, getting up in front of the patch of wheat she had landed in. Jason could see that she was struggling, so he pulled her up, making her turn red, then yank her hand away from his and turn her back to him.

Uh, you're welcome?

His Sense went off again and he walked towards a large, decrepit house about twenty feet away. Kalen walked past him to the abandoned house and examined it. All around the house there was an ominous purplish-black aura that looked like black smoke.

"You see what I see?" asked Kalen.

"Yeah, looks bad," said Jason.

"Looks like there's a nasty one in there somewhere," said Kalen.

Jason shuddered as they crept into the ghastly mist. The closer they got to the house, the more details Jason noticed—the weeds, the long-faded, egg-white paint job, and the cracks along the outer walls.

The door was ajar, and inside, aside from the

obvious signs of decay, it looked mostly furnished and untouched. The floors and inner walls had dark green clumps of … moss? Or mold? Mist swirled around the room. He could just barely make out a strange ornate object glistening in one of the corners. He was about to inspect it when a set of glowing eyes popped up from beneath the smoke.

"Did you see those *eyes*?!" he cried.

"Yeah … there's someone in there." Kalen ran into the smoke, Jason fearfully following behind her. Once inside the room, they felt the presence of the ghost grow more and more intense.

"Do you feel that, Jason? He's right here."

"Right *here*?!"

"Yes. His presence is overwhelming, isn't it?

"Yeah …" Jason shivered.

"Ready your weapon and keep your guar—"

Kalen paused. She turned her head slowly as a pair of shadowy, malevolent hands crawled up her back and then onto her shoulder. She jumped with a start. Then the hands clamped around her neck and engulfed her body, sending her up in the air. Kalen let out a muffled yelp. Jason ran forward.

"KALEN!!"

*   *   *

Gage hated Shadowmonsters for as long as he could remember. The "want to blow their damn heads off" kind of hate. He still had nightmares where he could hear his parents' screams as swarms of them ripped through them right in front of him. In the part of Brooklyn he lived in at the time, they were everywhere and he had to learn to fight back. Fast.

And he did.

The weapons he had honed from his own Spirit Energy had become his best friends, especially in the dangerous streets he lived in. After his parents' death, he had lived in youth homes and was tossed from foster home after foster home for years. The whole "I can see and fight ghosts" thing doesn't really fly in most households.

One day, he was taking on a large Shadowmonster that had been hunting him on the way home. The Samson couple had seen him hold his own against the behemoth, and then jumped in and helped him when he needed it. They told him that they had seen "potential" in him, and that they would take him in and let him fight all the ghosts he wanted.

Being adopted into a *rich* family was only the icing on the cake.

Being adopted into a rich family *who fought ghosts for a living* was more than he had ever dreamed of.

The last of the ghosts tormenting them had disintegrated, but he wasn't going to take any chances. "Trix, quick! We're almost to the Safe Room! There's probably more where those came from!" said Gage.

"Right," said Beatrice. They rushed to the secret door hidden in the walls of the hallway and waited as the door opened, then sprinted inside, Gage holding his handgun closely by his chest.

Gage and Beatrice rushed down the spiraling steps and into the chamber, which glowed from the tiles on the ground. In the center of the room, Beatrice held onto Gage tightly. He felt his cheeks heat up "It's alright. We'll be safe here," he said Gage and immediately began to recharge his Spirit Energy.

"Right. I can't sense anymore of them coming," said Beatrice.

Gage sighed. Orbs of energy emanated from his hands like light on a candle. "Weird … I swear I can still sense more of them."

"Hmm. Your Sense must still be stronger than mine," Beatrice said, looking down at the floor.

"Don't worry about it. Your Sense will grow stronger with experience," Gage reassured her. Suddenly, he gasped and grabbed Beatrice by the arm.

"What's wrong?" she asked.

"Come on! I think I know where she is!"

"Gage! What are you talking about? Wait!"

He pulled Beatrice by the arm and teleported

them both to where he seemed to have found his closest friend.

*   *   *

The abomination standing in front of Jason had a huge centipede-like body and a white mask of a face with at least eight black hollow eyes and a big black mouth. Great. Of course Jason had to deal with that in his first real fight as a Moderator! Its tentacle-like antenna had wrapped around Kalen's body, immobilizing her. How could she have let herself be blindsided by that? Thankfully, Jason stepped away from the monster, his head cocked to the side.

He readied his arrow, but as he was aiming, the monster's tail swept under him and tripped him. The monster then immediately body-slammed him. Kalen's heart skipped a beat and she let out a muffled cry while struggling to break free from it. Jason staggered back up and hid inside a hole in the wall. As he stumbled in, one of the centipede creature's antennae slithered around in the hole. From inside the hole, Jason shot an arrow at the tentacle and it broke off. The centipede monster recoiled and screeched in pain. Jason peeked out of the hole and aimed for the tentacles wrapped around Kalen.

The monster stopped screeching and lunged

at Jason again. He shot his arrow quickly. It missed! He made his way back inside the minute the monster reached the opening to the hole. The monster kept bashing its head at the opening. Then Kalen heard the banging of a gun. A shiver went down her spine as she sensed something very powerful moving in, closer and closer. The centipede monster was furious. It darted forward and wrapped its tentacles and Jason and picked him up, lifted him up high, then smacked him hard onto the ground.

Finally, Kalen was able to let out a burst of energy to break out of the centipede monster's clutches. She landed and helped Jason to his feet.

"Come on!" she cried, pulling his arm.

They quickly sprinted for the door, hand in hand, when Kalen saw an antenna swinging right towards them. She quickly parried it away with her rapier, but the impact knocked her to the ground and on her back. The monster crawled towards them, both of them vulnerable, but then something crashed through the ceiling. It suddenly shot at the monster with numerous bullets all over its body. Kalen glanced at their savior and dropped her jaw.

"Gage?!"

"Hurry up and get him out of here! I'll take care of Ugly over here!" he urged.

"By yourself?! Are you crazy? Let me—" Kalen started to protest.

"Out of the question! Get him outta here and take a pause for the cause!" he insisted.

Kalen hesitated for a moment, and then dragged an exhausted Jason out the door. She laid him out on the grass and sat beside him. His eyelids were fluttering closed. Beatrice ran out and formed a forcefield around the three of them.

"Thanks, Beatrice," Kalen panted, still confused.

Through the open door, Kalen watched as Gage readied his Spirit Fingers and dodged the centipede monster's swings and coils. He shot its arms, legs, and the many black eyes on its face. Then, he charged the gun's energy, let it grow larger, aimed straight for the finally tired monster, and fired.

"Open wide!" he yelled.

A large explosion filled the house. It began to crumble and fall apart. Kalen turned to the explosion and yelped. "Wait! Gage is still in there!" She jumped up to run in after him when she saw him shoot out of the chimney.

"Woo-hoo!" he shouted happily.

He landed a few feet from Jason, who had passed out and was now covered in debris, and Kalen, who stood there gaping, unable to move.

As soon as Gage caught up to them, he picked up on Kalen's demeanor and teased, "Hey, why the surprised look? Were you *worried* about me?"

Kalen snapped out of it, turned red, and pushed him. "No! I am *appalled* by your *idiocy*! You didn't have to blow the place up!"

"Who cares? It's an *abandoned* house." Gage shrugged with a bit of a smile on his face. Suddenly, he remembered that he was supposed to be mad at her.

"… like how you *abandoned* us after the movie *three* days ago and haven't been heard from since! Where the hell have you been?!"

"I'll explain later … Help me get him home, will you?" Kalen pointed to an unconscious Jason.

"What's he doing here, anyway? Oh, I get it. You ditched us for *him*." Gage scowled.

"Look," Kalen, with some exasperation, showed Gage the mark on Jason's hand, "He's a new Moderator and I was just showing him the ropes."

"Wait, you found out he was a Moderator *three days ago*?" Gage inquired.

"Two days ago, actually. And I've been helping him train ever since," Kalen said.

"How come you didn't tell me?" Gage asked indignantly.

Kalen paused for a moment then said, "I'm sorry. Everything happened so quickly, and I guess I got caught up with it all. I promise I won't flake like that ever again." Kalen wrapped her arms around

Gage.

He chuckled and said, "Alright, apology accepted. Why don't we take the dork to my place? James should be home. He's good with, like, first aid and stuff."

"Alright. Fine by me," said Kalen. She was so exhausted that she wasn't sure if her healing energy would even work right now.

CHAPTER 8

The sky over the ancient temple was an ominous mix of black, blue, and purple, with rain that could flood the city of Manhattan. Black shadows, long and thick even in the dark of night, enveloped its aged stone walls, radiating with malicious intent. Inside its foreboding walls, a man in black boots, a large dark brown hat, and a trench coat climbed to the top of a grand flight of stairs to where a large purple-and-black entity awaited.

"Master, forgive me. I have failed to retrieve the Pandora's Box. My centipede minion was defeated," the man said. "Three Moderators—an archer, a swordswoman, and a gunslinger—entered and destroyed the remains of the abandoned home, so my centipede was not able to search and retrieve it."

"Most disappointing," the large black entity said calmly, but with a twinge of disappointment in its voice. "Those children are becoming a bit of a problem. They must be taken care of immediately if my plan is to come to fruition."

"Yes. What are your orders, Master?" the man in the trench coat asked, his long black hair swishing from his face, which was partially covered by his hat.

"For now, your orders are to enter into the world of the mortals, disguise yourself as one of them, then find that artifact!"

"Yes, Master," the man in the trench coat said, his pale, monstrous face morphing into a more human-looking one with shorter black hair, fair, flawless skin, and radiant reddish-black eyes.

*   *   *

Jason's head was pounding and his body felt heavy when he came to. "Is this what a hangover feels like?" he wondered. He sat up on a couch he didn't recognize, where his eyes met those of a very fair-skinned man with a short, neat blonde buzz cut.

"Oh, good. You're awake," the man said softly.

"Huh? Who are you?" Jason asked faintly.

"I'm James Samson; Gage's father," the man answered.

"Gage's father?" Jason echoed. He tensed up and sat up straight.

"Ha ha, I see that you're new to the group. He tends to get off on the wrong foot with a lot of people, but I assure you, once he's known you long enough, he'll start warming up to you."

Jason relaxed a bit. He looked around the large, high-ceilinged room, which was filled with modern, bold tapestries and furniture.

"Where am I, anyway?" he asked.

"Why, you're in my home, of course," James replied.

Jason tensed up again, realizing that meant he was in the Samson Manor, as in the "Samson Mobile" Samsons. It was a penthouse on the Upper East Side, but everyone called it the Samson Manor. Kalen had told him that Gage was a foster child. Of all the families to get adopted into, Gage got adopted by the *Samsons*.

"Like I said, he'll warm up to you eventually. I can feel it. You seem like a nice boy." James chuckled reassuringly.

Then an image flashed in his mind—Gage randomly swooping in from out of nowhere and blowing up the centipede monster just to show off to Kalen and make him look bad! Though, he *did* save him from certain death. The least he could do was thank him. He got up from the couch. "Thanks, Mr. Samson. I think I'll go find him and the others now."

"I'm glad to hear that. I'm not quite sure where they are. You're welcome to look for them and while you're at it, take a look around." James said.

Jason walked down the long, red carpeted hallways. peering about as he went. Just before the stairway, he saw a magnificent large glass chandelier dangling from above, the many modern abstract paintings and unusual sculptures, and wine cabinets that lined the halls—a sharp contrast to the old-fashioned decoration and rustic greenery that engulfed Kalen's home.

As he continued down the hallway past the stairs, he noted that the door to one of the rooms was slightly ajar and decided to have a look. A king-sized bed in the middle of the back wall was made up with red-and-black-striped bedding. It was surprisingly neat, though Jason did notice some clothes lying about. J-rock and K-Pop posters dominated much of the walls, which were painted red like much of the house.

"This must be Gage's room."

On the dresser were a wooden carving of a geisha holding a parasol and a wooden music box with dragons carved on its sides. He walked over to music box and took it from its place to sit on the bed with it.

I wonder what Gage would be doing with something like this, Jason thought to himself.

He opened it and twisted the knob on the side of it. The music box tinkled a soothing, uplifting melody, and the little dragons inside the box spun around to the music. The simple beauty of the tune warmed Jason up inside as though the music box was a source of positive energy meant to lighten the spirit.

Then Jason muttered to himself, "Maybe that's why Gage has this thing; Something from his childhood to cheer him up."

From his real parents.

That thought made him frown. He put the music box back exactly where he found it, or at least where he remembered finding it, and hurried out of the room. If Gage ever suspected that he messed with it, who knows what he'd do.

Jason walked out of Gage's room, down the stairs, and past the long dining room table, when he thought he could hear humming and singing. Jason followed the sound of the humming into one of the rooms. The room Jason had walked into was full of wine bottles, some full and in shelves, other corked and on the side tables, and barely visible wine-red stains on the carpet. He followed the humming to the kitchen door. Peering inside, he saw a tall, burgundy-haired woman leaning over the stove, who seemed to be baking pumpkin cookies with Beatrice.

Beatrice turned to him and said in a surprised voice, "Oh, Jason, you're awake!"

"Yeah," Jason replied, then looking at the burgundy-haired woman with a confused look, "You must be Mrs. Samson?"

"Hi! Call me Jessica," she greeted him extravagantly, maybe even drunkenly. "And who might *you* be, child? Would you by any chance be my son's boyfriend?"

Jason jumped in shock looking visibly bewildered. *What?* Me*? His* boyfriend*? This lady must be off her rocker!*

Beatrice got between them and stammered, "No, no! This is Jason, one of Kalen's friends." She turned to Jason and said formally, "And yes, this is Jessica Samson, Gage's foster mother."

"Ah, she's told us *a lot* about you." Jessica chuckled. Then Beatrice's hand clamped over her mouth, startling the older woman. Murmuring came from the other room.

"What's that over there?" Jason pointed to a large brass fountain with a carving of a fairy on it.

"Oh, that? That's the imported absinthe fountain I ordered last week! You like it? It looks like a fairy!" Jessica chirped.

"I don't talk about him a lot!" Kalen snapped, entering the room with Gage.

"Yeah, ya do!" Gage commented from behind her before turning to his adoptive mother. "So there you are! I see you've been drinkin' again. Honestly, is every day a party to you?"

"Yep! These are about done. Kiddos, follow me to my quarters!" Jessica said waving her arms around with a flourish.

The group followed her down a corridor to the left. "So, Jason, where are you from?" Jessica slurred loudly.

"Staten Island," he answered meekly.

"What was that?! *Speak up*!" Jessica barked out.

"He said he lives in Staten Island, Jess," Gage said almost as loudly.

"Ah! So, you're a Moderator now, huh? You go on any dangerous missions yet?" Jessica said, getting in his face and grinning like the Cheshire cat, making him feel a little unsettled.

"Yeah, the one that landed me here ..." Jason chuckled nervously.

"Oh, that was your first mission, eh? Don't beat yourself up! Lots of people bomb on their first mission! Besides, a little birdie told me you held your own for a while out there!" Jessica said before patting Jason's back rather roughly, then turning to a blushing Kalen. "Next stop: the Safe Room! *Choo choo*!" She herded them out of the room and tried to jump on Gage's back.

"Whoa, there!" Gage grunted, then sighed, and ended up giving his own mother a piggyback ride, "Really gotta lay off the wine ..."

"Safe Room?" Jason asked.

"It's what we call our chunk of the Chamber of Energy. I just like calling it the Safe Room 'cause it sounds more badass! You know, like, 'Hurry! They'll never reach us in the Safe Room!'" said Gage enthusiastically.

"Ha ha! Yeah, it does sound pretty

awesome!" Jason agreed.

"Yeah," they both sighed.

Then they snapped out of it, remembering that they were supposed to hate each other, and turned away from each other in a huff.

Kalen watched this and let out an exasperated groan.

Jessica walked into the Chamber of Energy and spread her arms out, making a giant circle from her Spirit Energy. The white circle floated up into the center of the room and turned on like a television.

"Huh? What did she just do?!" Jason said, turning to Kalen.

"She used her Spirit Energy to create a projector to contact my mother," said Kalen.

"She knows your mom?" asked Jason.

"Oh, she and I are old friends from high school!" Jessica smiled. Suddenly, Mrs. Morrigan's face appeared on the screen, making Jason jump.

"Hey, Candace!" said Jessica, drawing out her words.

"Jessica! How are you, hon?" Mrs. Morrigan replied unusually happily.

"Oh, I just called to say your daughter's come back just fine!"

"And how did Jason and Kalen do on the mission?" asked Mrs. Morrigan.

"Oh, they did great!" Jessica replied, waving

her hand casually. "My Gage helped them out as well!"

"Good, good!" Mrs. Morrigan smiled.

Just then, Jason's ringtone started blaring. He visibly cringed as the main menu music to "Tomes and Togas" began to play in his front pocket.

"The hell is that?" Gage chuckled.

"Why does that sound familiar?" Kalen mused.

"I'll be right back guys. It's probably my mom checking on me."

"Understood, Jason, take your time," Mrs. Morrigan nodded, while Jessica waved him away.

Jason tiptoed out of the room and, when he reached someplace quiet, pulled out his phone. The caller ID read "Dimi."

"Dude! You're alive! About time you picked up!" Dimitria hissed on the other line.

"Hey, Dimi. I'm at … Gage's house, oddly enough?"

"Gage's house? What the fu—? Why are you at Gage's house? I thought—"

"Look, it's a long story. I'll tell you all about it when I get home."

"You fucking better! Jason—"

Beep! Jason hung up the phone and rushed back into the living room. He felt a pang of guilt for having to hang up on and keep his best friend out of the loop like that but Jason was so overwhelmed by everything that had happened, he needed some breathing room before he could explain it to anyone.

*   *   *

The man in the trench coat walked down the dark and treacherous Manhattan streets, the moon in plain view, even with all of the city lights. He walked across the street without a word into the fray of the traffic. Horns honked and people yelled, but he made no reaction. He fixed his gaze on a large building with a gated fence. It was easily ten feet tall, but he scrambled up and then jumped from the top without hesitation, landing with graceful ease. Straightening up, he walked into the property's front lawn, passing a sign that read Dwayne Whitewood High.

As he walked toward the building, he was greeted halfway by a man dressed in a suit.

"Can I help you, sir?"

"Actually, I'm here to apply for a job," the man said, his reddish-black, catlike eyes gleaming through the splits of his wild black bangs.

*   *   *

Jason woke up early to the sound of his

alarm clock. It was 5:40 a.m. He groaned, turned it off, and went back to sleep. He had been through a lot. He needed a break. What felt like moments later, his cell phone rang.

Loudly.

He groaned and got up again to pick up his phone. It was Kalen. What did Kalen want so early in the morning? He picked up the phone and said groggily, "Hello?"

"Hey! Wake up!" she said. "You're gonna be late for school!"

"Kalen??" Jason said, still caught off guard.

"Yeah, it's *me*! *Hurry up,* idiot!" Kalen said irately.

"Oh crap! What time is it?!" Jason said, shocked.

"It's 6:45!" Kalen replied. "You're usually nearly here by now, yeah? And you haven't even left your house?"

"*6:45?!* On my way!" Jason said.

It sucked that Jason still hadn't gotten the hang of the teleportation technique yet. Kalen had said before he went home the other day that he'd need a lot of rest and a lot more training to learn that. He slipped on his black school uniform polo shirt, navy-blue school uniform pants, and his red sneakers and tried to teleport to the front of the school anyway, too flustered to even think about breakfast.

He felt lightheaded and laid on the ground for a moment to collect himself. Boy, Kalen was right. This did take a lot of energy. He looked around, glancing at the sign saying "Dwayne Whitewood High", and hustled over to the front entrance.

*   *   *

Kalen was tapping her foot impatiently as she stood in front of the school's gate waiting for Jason to arrive. She looked up at the sky.

"You can't baby him forever. Guys hate that." Gage bent down in front of her with a smirk. Beatrice leaned on one of the school's freshly planted trees next to them.

Kalen stuck her tongue out. "I'm not! I'm just a little concerned, that's all."

Just then, a crow swooped down. Kalen extended an arm, where it perched itself. Kalen gave it an inquisitive stare, to which the crow responded with a single nod of its head. She then let out a sigh of relief and mumbled, "Good. He's coming soon," in a voice low enough that she thought she couldn't be heard.

Gage popped up next to her wearing an exasperated glare. "Really? You sent your crow over to check on him? Like you used to do to me in *middle school*? C'mon, Kalen!" he accused.

"I was concerned!" Kalen cried, her face beet red.

And it was only for a couple of weeks after you nearly got us killed by that snake monster in Lake Champlain.

*   *   *

He looked at the sign again and read: "Dwayne Whitewood High: Next Seven Blocks." Then, he let out an irritated groan and tromped down the pavement.

It was hard to believe he was able to get into a prestigious school in Manhattan like Whitewood High. When he got accepted, his mother had insisted that he go, no matter how expensive. She only wanted the best education for her son, and for him to get away from the bullies at his last school. And they were doing their best to make it work. He and his mother worked together at the pizzeria just three blocks from the school.

"Hey! Took you long enough!" Kalen said, sounding less irate in person than she had on the phone. "Come on!" She grabbed his and Gage's hands and sped off to the door, Beatrice running closely behind.

The first class was homeroom. The four of them all sat together, close to the windows, a first; normally Jason stared at the back of Kalen's head from the last row. The teacher, a skinny, stern-looking man with gelled-back hair and small round glasses, droned on and on about the history of the Pythagorean theorem.

Gage was slumped in his chair in utter boredom, his square, black bangs dangling over his tired eyes. He mouthed an exaggerated yawn to Sandro, sitting one row across from him. Sandro let out a stifled laugh.

Beatrice giggled, and then quickly shushed them nervously. Kalen merely rolled her eyes, glanced at Jason in the seat across from her, and then went back to writing notes.

Gage continued to make funny faces at the teacher when he wasn't looking, while Sandro stifled laughs while trying to shut him up at the same time. Then the teacher turned around and finally caught them in the act.

"Ahem! Mr. Samson! Mr. Pereira! Is there something you would like to share with the class?" he asked irately.

"Yeah, Mr. Wes, I think I do," Gage replied, and then he cried out in exasperation, "This class is so stupid!"

Sandro couldn't hold back anymore; he let out a hysterical, uncontrollable laugh, as did most of the class. Beatrice blushed profusely, while Kalen rolled her eyes at them, and Jason smacked his forehead into his hand in disbelief.

Mr. Wes, appalled, said to Gage, "Well, if this class is so 'stupid' to you, you are free to go entertain yourself *in the principal's office*!"

Gage snickered and said "Okay, fine by me!" He hopped happily to his feet and grabbed his stuff before practically skipping to the door.

Sandro whispered, "Valeu, amigo!"

Just then, Jason's stomach grumbled—loudly. Everyone in the classroom, even Gage, who hadn't left the room yet, stared at him.

The class again burst into hysterical laughter.

Jason turned bright red and let out an embarrassed chuckle. He was in such a rush to leave home that he had forgotten to get breakfast.

"You! Making inappropriate noises in the classroom, and then laughing about it! You go to the principal's office as well!" yelled Mr. Wes.

"But, but …," Jason stammered.

"But, Mr. Wes, he didn't do anything wrong!" Kalen defended him.

"No buts! Principal's office *now*!" yelled Mr. Wes.

"Yes, Mr. Wes," Jason said dejectedly.

"Sorry, Jason. See you at lunch." Kalen whispered to him as he got up, grabbed his belongings, and left.

Jason walked to the door, joining a smirking Gage when Mr. Wes said, "Samson! Walker! What are you standing around for? Go, already!"

Gage gave him a military salute and walked out the door, Jason following him, though making sure to stay a few steps behind.

The door had shut behind them, and Mr. Wes turned to the class and said, "Well, as I was saying: the hypotenuse is equal to …" Kalen, Beatrice, and Sandro exchanged glances and sighed in discontent.

*   *   *

The two boys walked down the halls when Jason turned to Gage and asked, "Um, where exactly *is* the principal's office?"

"You're kidding, right?" Gage groaned, making Jason chuckle nervously, before saying, "Well, I guess that's to be expected from a sheltered goody-goody like you, huh? Follow me. I happen to be a regular there."

He took the lead and let the lost little boy follow him along. A building and a few flights of stairs later, they had made it to a door with a few chairs set up in front of it.

"Well, here we are. Don't be shy; have a seat," Gage said sardonically.

The two of them sat down in the chairs until a neatly dressed woman came out, the annoying receptionist. "So, Gage," she greeted him familiarly.

"I hear you've been giving Mr. Wes a hard time again. Who's your friend?"

"He's *not* my *friend*," both boys growled.

"Well, anyway, the principal will be ready for you in a few minutes," the woman said sweetly, and then went back inside the room.

"She seemed nice." Jason smiled.

"Shut up," said Gage.

The clock above them ticked. Several minutes went by.

Jason's stomach grumbled loudly again.

"Sorry …," said Jason.

Five more minutes went by.

"A few minutes my ass," Gage complained.

"It is taking a long time," said Jason. His stomach grumbled again.

Another five minutes went by.

Jason's stomach grumbled even louder.

"Sorry. I was in such a rush this morning, I forgot to get breakfast," said Jason.

Gage let out an exasperated sigh. He couldn't stand the kid, but he also couldn't sit through another minute of the grating noise.

He reached into his backpack, pulled out a candy bar, and handed it to Jason. "Here. Have this."

"Um … thanks …," said Jason, the beginning of a smile forming.

Gage's cheeks felt annoyingly warm, but he

recovered quickly and said in a mocking tone, "'*Um … thanks …*' Geez! Just take it already!" Jason did just that and ate it voraciously.

Stupid kid, Gage thought to himself.

A minute or so later, the receptionist appeared again. "The principal is ready to speak with you two now."

CHAPTER 9

"**C**ome, come. Sit," said the principal, who furrowed his brow at the boys.

"Yes sir," the boys replied. They sat down on the chairs in front of his desk. "So, Gage. Taunting Mr. Wes again, are we?" the principal asked.

Gage let out something along the lines of either a playful giggle or a nervous titter.

"What am I going to do with you? You can't just go around scuffling with anyone who irritates you. You need a better way to resolve your problems. I think you should have a talk with our school's guidance counselor."

"Wait, what? We have a guidance counselor?" Gage asked.

He couldn't help but roll his eyes. *Great, not another guidance counselor. This is going to be like middle school all over again.*

"Yes. We just hired him. He is coming in right now."

"Right now, huh?" Gage asked.

"And as for you …" The principal leered at Jason. "What's your name, son?"

"Jason, sir. Jason Walker," Jason replied

quietly.

"Well, I haven't seen you before, but stay out of trouble, lest you end up like him." The principal glared at Gage, who had been humming a tune.

Then a man with long black hair down to his chin and piercing black eyes walked in and stood by the door.

"So, this is the boy you wanted me to see?"

"Yes. This is him. Please get through to him! I'm *begging* you!" The principal clasped his hands together in prayer position.

"Come with me, then," the man said to Gage. Gage got up from his seat and followed the man out the door. They reached a door with a gold plate on the front that read Dr. Adel's Office.

"Right this way. Come in," Dr. Adel said to Gage. The man smiled and sat at his desk. "Have a seat," he said politely.

Ha! He thinks he can be all nice-guy to get through to me? What an idiot! Gage thought.

"'Kay," he replied in a surly manner, accepting the seat offered to him.

"Now, Gage. Tell me a bit about your family," Dr. Adel said, clasping his fingers together.

Gage took a deep breath and sighed. Gage couldn't help but feel drained, like something was sucking the life force out of him.

"Well, I have a mom and a dad. Their names

are Jessica and James …," he began warily.

"Okay. What does your family do for a living?"

"Well, my dad owns a cell phone company called Samson Mobile, and my mom is a lawyer," said Gage. He wasn't exactly lying. Yes, his foster parents were Moderators, but they *did* have day jobs.

Dr. Adel's droopy lids perked with curiosity. "I see. What do *you* like to do?" he asked.

"Um … I just hang around the city with my friends," said Gage as he shuffled around in his seat.

Then Dr. Adel raised a brow and asked, "What do you *do* with your friends?"

"Stuff …"

At this point, it seemed it was taking all Dr. Adel had to remain polite. "What *kind* of stuff?"

"You know, just hang out, mess around, party, and buy stuff … you know, just … *stuff* …"

"I see … Well, it looks like you're not feeling like talking, so I'll let you out early for now …" Dr. Adel sighed, rubbing at his temples. His friendly smile was wearing off.

"Well, thanks. That's real cool of you, Doc," Gage said, his eyes lighting up. As he was about to leave, he started to feel dizzy.

"Anytime you're ready to come and *really* talk …," Dr. Adel began.

Gage turned around and asked, "Yeah?"

"… Remember this face …" At that moment, Dr. Adel's voice began to echo in Gage's ear, making him start. His dizziness worsened, and he shut the door behind him and staggered down the hallway to his next class.

"Remember this face …"

Where have I heard that before? Gage thought. *Come to think of it, the guy himself kinda reminds me of someone. I just can't put my finger on* whom … He rubbed his blue eyes and turned to Jason, who had apparently been sent to see the counselor too and was waiting for his turn.

"Go on ahead. He's actually pretty cool," Gage smiled, staggering past him.

"You okay? You don't look so good," Jason said to his frenemy.

"I'm fine. Just a little dizzy. I'll just get some water or something on the way to class," he replied.

"Okay, see ya," Jason said hesitantly.

He walked into Dr. Adel's office and was greeted with, "Ah, Mr. Walker. Sit down. Let's have a chat, shall we?"

He seems nice, just like Gage said, Jason thought.

He sat in the chair in front of the black-haired man's desk. He gulped, and then looked into his dark, hypnotic eyes with his own timid, hazel eyes. Jason couldn't help but feel uneasy under the man's overpowering gaze.

"Tell me something about yourself," he said to Jason.

Suddenly, Jason felt drained. Then he saw black mist floating around Dr. Adel. The mist danced around his neck, onto the desk, and then drew closer and closer to Jason's face. It felt like a hundred tiny hands were grasping at him, trying to choke him to death.

As it drew closer to him, he heard a faint, tiny voice say, "I'm hungry. When can I eat him?"

Jason felt his stomach go rock hard. He panicked and scanned the room for the source of the voice. Instead, he looked into his own eyes in a reflection in the window; they were glowing yellow. Out of the corner of his eye, he saw a blinding flash of red coming from Dr. Adel's direction. Jason jumped back in fear. Then the black mist disappeared.

"Mr. Walker, are you all right?" Dr. Adel asked in a concerned tone.

"Yeah ...," Jason said weakly.

"You look pale ...," Dr. Adel said with a slight smirk, his eyes starting to glisten red.

Jason jumped up and said, "U-um ... I-I gotta go!" And with that, he ran out the door. Jason huffed and puffed down the hallway after Gage, but there was no sign of him. Something was *not* right about this guy, and he had to tell someone. But it looked like he wouldn't be able to meet up with the whole gang until lunchtime.

*　　*　　*

Dr. Adel sat on his desk smirking as he pulled out a rustic-looking mirror shaped like a seashell. Then his reflection in the mirror went black and a pair of glowing, malevolent purple eyes shone in the mirror.

"What is the meaning of this insubordination? How dare you deny me those souls?" the mirror asked.

"It's only because you asked me to infiltrate the school to get rid of that group of troublesome Moderators. Besides, if people started dying this soon and this randomly, it would cause a massive panic."

"But you must not forget your ultimate duty: To feed me the souls of those that are enduring intense struggle and despair. When the time comes, you must summon your monsters into the world to reap the souls of those humans and bring them to me. Do not disappoint me," said the monster in the mirror.

"I will not, Master," said the man named Moros, his eyes glowing red again. And with that the blackness in the mirror dissipated and Moros's reflection appeared again.

"Ahhh, how I missed this form. My eyes look dazzling in this light," he said to himself haughtily.

CHAPTER 10

It was lunchtime and Jason had just gotten his freshly made spaghetti and meatballs, crème brûlée with whipped cream and a strawberry, and iced tea. The cafeteria food was definitely one of the perks of Whitewood High. He walked down the rows of tables, looking for a familiar face among the crowd of snooty, aloof strangers.

Suddenly, he heard Kalen shout out, "Hey, Jason! Over here!"

Jason rushed over to get a seat across from his red-headed crush and said, "Hey! Food today is good, huh?"

Kalen said rather matter-of-factly while grazing her food, "Of course it's 'good'; the school's food *is* prepared by professional chefs."

Gage scoffed so hard he nearly choked on his salmon. "Ugh! How can you say that so casually?! This is probably the best salmon and mashed potatoes I've ever eaten! I swear ... damn rich people," he scolded while stuffing his face just a chair away from Jason, and across from Beatrice.

"You're rich, too, idiot," Kalen informed him with a glazed stare.

"Not by birth. That's not the point, though!

Not everyone gets to have this kind of food every day! At the group home, *orphanage*, whatever you wanna call it, we had so little, burglars would feel sorry for us and leave us stuff instead of stealin' ours."

Jason did a double-take. Gage actually seemed sincere in his aggravation, not being sarcastic or condescending.

"Just saying, you don't have to be snobby about it, even if it is *Jason*." Gage rolled his eyes as he uttered his name.

"So, how was your trip to the principal's office?" Kalen asked sympathetically.

"Well, Gage and I had to talk to this guidance counselor guy named Dr. Adel. He seems nice and polite but …" Jason leaned in closer to the others to whisper, "Listen, I started talking to the guy and all of sudden I started to feel drained and dizzy. Gage felt it, too! Right?"

"Uh … yeah. Actually, that was a little weird," said Gage.

"And his eyes glowed red!" Jason continued.

"Whoa, whoa, whoa! *That* I didn't see coming! Are you sure you weren't getting delirious from hunger or something, kid?" Gage replied.

As if on cue, Jason's stomach started to grumble.

"Dude, eat something already!" Gage

ordered.

"Don't *yell* at him!" Kalen scolded him.

"But I wasn't …," Gage started to say, but instead let out an exasperated sigh and then said, "Ugh, go on."

"I also saw smoke coming from his body, a-and it *talked*! I heard it! It—" Before Jason could finish his sentence, Kalen shoved a fork full of Gage's salmon into his mouth, making Gage laugh loudly.

A prefect walking by the table swatted Gage on the back of the head and barked, "Quiet! No loud laughter in the cafeteria!"

"Man, I swear, this has to be the only school in the country with fuckin' *prefects* walkin' around everywhere," Gage grumbled, rubbing the back of his head, his Brooklyn accent thickening again. He then turned to the prefect to yell, "And I'm pretty sure corporal punishment in schools was banned, like, decades ago!"

"Alright, that's enough out of you! I agree with Gage. You were probably delusional with hunger. Keep eating," Kalen sighed.

"But I swear I saw … I guess you're right …," Jason said, turning to his lunch.

*   *   *

After school, Jason and Kalen were walking

ahead of Beatrice down the stairs at the front entrance when Kalen leaned to Jason and said, blushing, "So, Jason, wanna hang out at my house for a while? Y-you know, to go over the *mountain* of math homework we have in Mr. Wes's class?"

"*Oh crap*! What was the assignment? I was sent to the principal's office before he assigned it!" Jason panicked.

Kalen chuckled and said, "I'll tell you when we get to my house."

"Great! Oh! I need to get my math textbook out of my locker! Be right back!" said Jason, rushing back into the school. Kalen stood in place, watching him run inside. Then Beatrice walked by and, forgetting she was there, Kalen made a startled jump.

She turned to her blonde friend and said, "Beatrice … can I tell you a secret?"

"Sure, what is it?" asked Beatrice with a sweet expression on her face.

"I've never kissed a boy before," Kalen said, turning bright red.

"Wait, didn't you tell Gage that you kissed a guy you were dating once?"

"I only said it to get him off my back." Kalen started fidgeting with her bangs.

Kalen had the feeling that someone was behind them. Then a familiar voice said in a sing-song voice, "I can hear you!"

The girls were so startled, they almost jumped out of their shoes.

"Gage!" Kalen cried, "You scared the hell out of us!" Then she scanned his face and detected a slight smile. "You heard what I was saying, didn't you?" she said in a panic, then shoved him lightly and threatened, "*Don't* laugh …"

Gage chuckled and said, "I wasn't gonna! Trust me! And I won't say anything to your Prince Charming, Jason, either."

"What is that supposed to … You *better* not!" Kalen growled, her cheeks reddening.

"I won't, I promise!"

Gage smiled, but Kalen knew him too well. She could still see a glimmer of hurt in his eyes. She started to apologize for keeping things from him when Gage abruptly turned to cross the street.

"Gage! Watch out! You could get hit by cars!" Beatrice cried out.

"I'll be fine! I'm just gonna grab a bite to eat at a place a few blocks away!"

"O-okay! Come home soon, though! Mr. Wes assigned us some homework after you left!" Beatrice yelled out to him.

"Pffft! Bah! *That* jerk again? Can't stand him …"

"Gage! Watch out!" Beatrice yelled again.

Gage turned to his left and saw a black motorcycle seemingly driving straight at him. He quickly jumped to the sidewalk on the other side, the motorcycle not stopping for a second.

"Hey! Watch it!" Gage yelled angrily, his fist in the air. He watched the motorcycle drive away, and then continued to head down the sidewalk, lifting a hand to wave goodbye to his two friends.

*   *   *

"Welcome back, Jason," Mrs. Morrigan said with a smile as Jason and Kalen walked in the door.

"Hello, Mrs. Morrigan," said Jason.

"Come in! Come in!" Mrs. Morrigan said in an unusually friendly tone.

I've never seen her so friendly ... Jason thought.

He smiled and walked inside the living room. The two teens walked up the stairs to the private library, which was lined with ten-foot-tall bookshelves, and in the corner sat a brown leather couch with a small table next to it for them to put their books. They dropped their backpacks on the floor and Jason sat down.

"I'll be right back. I'm going to get some snacks, if that's alright with you," said Kalen.

"Yeah! Great!" said Jason.

"'Kay, be right back." Kalen smiled and walked out of the room.

Jason stayed seated on the couch, removed his black school uniform sweater, and put it in his backpack. He leaned back onto the couch, wobbling a bit as he misjudged the depth of it, and waited. A few minutes later, Kalen returned to the room with a trayful of jumbo shrimp and dip and an older, paler-skinned man in a black tuxedo following behind her.

"Ah, that shrimp looks good! Oh, who's that?" Jason asked, moving his head towards the man in the tuxedo.

"Oh, this is our butler, Harold. Harold, this is my friend, Jason."

The man bowed and said, with a hint of a British accent, "Pleasure to meet you, Jason."

Jason scrambled up and, bowing his head awkwardly, said, "Nice to meet you, too!" He wasn't quite sure how to act around Kalen's butler, not having seen one before except in the movies.

"I hope you two enjoy your meal. I must attend to the garden now; the azaleas haven't been watered in quite some time," Harold the butler said as he made his way to the door.

"Okay. Good luck with that," Jason said, attempting to sound appreciative.

After the butler left, Kalen took her math book out of her backpack and Jason did the same. "Okay let's get started, shall we?" said Kalen.

"Yeah. I'm going to need some help, though

… Trig is *not* my strong suit," Jason replied.

Kalen teasingly rolled her eyes and laughed. "Gage isn't exactly a mathematician himself, so don't be too worried now."

Jason laughed at that as well, and with that, they opened their books and started on their homework. About an hour and a half of joking and jumbo shrimp to lighten the mood, Jason felt like the math homework wasn't the only thing that was moving forward. At Kalen's suggestion, mumbling something about Harold watering the garden, the two put their things away and walked out to the west wing, where the azalea garden was. They sat side by side on a wooden bench by a fountain surrounded by azalea bushes, sprinkled with drops of the water from the fountain.

"It sure is beautiful out, huh?" Kalen leaned forward, her ivory, freckled skin glowing in the late afternoon light.

"Yeah!" Jason replied, with a hint of nervousness in his voice, leaning in as she did.

"Look at that sunset! It's so … perfect … don't you agree?" she asked.

Jason looked at the sky, with its swirls of orange, yellow, pink, and red, and said, "It's very beautiful …" Now he was looking at her and not the sky.

"Jason? Could you lean in a little closer …? I need to tell you something …?" Kalen asked.

They both leaned in even closer, their lips just two inches apart. Jason started to tremble in anticipation. Then as their lips were about to touch …

 Z-zing!

 "Ahhh!"

 "Augh!"

Both of their Spirit Energies suddenly went berserk. Jason's skull tingled, revealing a blurred image of a young girl. Then, he saw a large building covered with vines and flower buds. It was most likely abandoned. He knew Kalen saw the same thing.

 "What the heck was that?" Jason groaned.

 "Spirit Sense. Another spirit has manifested. This one is an innocent spirit," Kalen said in a rather disappointed tone.

 "Wow, what an alarm system. If only my alarm clock for school was this effective," Jason said, equally disappointed. "I-I guess we should go, then …"

 "Hang on. Let me get a handle on its location." Kalen rubbed her temples for a minute. "It's in the school."

 "'In the school'?" Jason asked warily.

 "Yeah, it's an old school. Lots of spirits come there. You *just* uncovered your abilities, so you wouldn't have noticed, but they've been hanging around for longer than you or I have. A lot of them are innocent, though. They won't be like that thing we saw in Staten Island."

Relief washed over Jason.

Kalen continued. "Remember, there are two kinds of spirits we specialize in: the Innocent ones, ones that have recently died and still look human; and the Tainted ones, tainted with *what* we don't know yet, and they *don't* look human, like the ones we saw before, the Shadowmonsters. The Innocents usually need our help. And that's what we're going to do now."

Kalen quickly grabbed Jason's hand, making his cheeks flush, and they instantly teleported to the school.

*   *   *

The school looked very different at night than it did in the day. The bright, distinguished building was now murky, dark, and foreboding. There was a strange aura that emanated from inside and out of the school. Jason walked towards the entrance door and tried to open it.

"Crap! Locked," he complained.

"Duh! The school always closes up at night," Kalen rebuked.

"How're we going to get inside?" asked Jason.

"I'll tell you how we're getting inside!" said

a familiar voice. Jason and Kalen turned back to see Gage standing behind them. Then, he pointed upward, at the windows.

"We'll climb in through the front window!" he said with a smile.

"How? The windows are all locked shut by the security system!" said Kalen, "What are you doing here, anyway?" Kalen sensed Gage flinch at that comment.

He replied, frowning and turning his head defensively, "What do you mean? It's my job, ain't it?"

Kalen also flinched and said, "Right, sorry."

That didn't change his expression much. She tried to change the subject by asking, "So, what's the plan?"

Gage walked over to a piece of brick by the one of the walls and picked it up from the ground.

"Hmm, convenient."

He walked over to the front door examined the knob.

"No! You're not!" Kalen yelled.

"You can't be serious!" said Jason.

"Oh, but I am!" Gage smirked.

"But you'd be destroying school property!" Jason yelled.

"Oh, *grow a pair!*" Gage groaned. "No one who ever amounted to anything important ever got where they were by always playin' it safe, always playin' by the rules. Desperate times call for desperate measures!" He gained the momentum he needed to thrust the brick at the doorknob.

Clank! Clank! Clank!

After pounding the knob with the brick several times, the knob broke off and the door slid open slightly. Gage gave a thumbs-up, signaling that the coast was clear. He swung the door open and went inside, the others following close behind.

"We are gonna get in *so* much trouble if we get caught," Jason said.

Gage groaned, "Don't be such a baby! We're not gonna get caught!"

"I can sense the energy getting stronger. It might be coming from upstairs. Let's split up and find the spirit," said Kalen.

"Really? *Split up*? Why can't we just check it out together? You know, so that way whatever's in there can't pick us off one by one," Jason suggested.

"Relax. This isn't a horror movie. We'll be fine!" Kalen reassured him.

The three of them—Jason, reluctantly so—split up and searched for the spirit emanating the powerful energy. They agreed Kalen would check the second floor, Jason the third, and Gage the fourth floor, with the faculty offices, and the roof.

Kalen walked through the hall, carefully

tracing the energy and tracking the source of it down. She touched the first door and it glowed as her Spirit Energy channeled from her body to the door. She closed her eyes and concentrated on searching for the energy through the door.

Nope. Nothing, Kalen thought.

Then she checked the second door.

Still nothing.

BANG!

What was that?! Kalen thought.

"Ow," she heard someone mumble.

*   *   *

Up on the third floor, Jason had run a bit too quickly and slipped on a puddle by the boy's bathroom.

"Ow," he groaned.

He got up to his feet, and then grumbled, "Of all the floors, why'd *I* have to get the slippery one? Why couldn't *Gage* get the slippery one?"

Just then, he looked at the puddle and noticed that the water in the puddle was growing. He slowly walked into the boys' bathroom. The door made a loud creak when it opened. He tiptoed inside, scanning the room for anything suspicious. Then he felt the hem of his jeans get wet. He walked further inside and looked toward the sinks. One of them was overflowing. Someone had left it running.

Geez, the nerve of some people! Leaving the sink running all this time, he thought.

He turned the faucet, shutting the water off, and walked out the door, and then heard the sound of water rushing again. He turned to see that the sink behind him was still off, but another sink a few feet away had been turned on! He walked over to that sink and turned it off. This repeated for several minutes, until Jason heard a faint giggle. It echoed through the room and straight back into his ears in a way that made the hairs on his arms and back of his head stand upright.

"What was that?" He panicked and ran out of the bathroom. As he bent down to catch his breath, the giggling got louder.

Footsteps.

Jason whimpered. He tugged at the tops of his hair as he speedwalked down the halls.

"Hey, you, over there. With the Dwayne Whitewood High uniform. Could you please help me?" a docile disembodied voice called out.

He slowly turned around and behind him was a girl who looked about his age. She was pale and washed out and was wearing the school's uniform. "Help me, please," she whispered so quietly, Jason could barely hear her.

He jumped and let out a loud scream. "Aahh! Ghost girl!" he yelled out while running as fast as he could down the halls.

Wait, of course it's a ghost! This is part of my job, too, Jason thought.

He turned back to the ghost girl with the uniform and said, "Hey, sorry for the little outburst just now … I'm kinda new to the job."

"Oh, it's alright. I'm used to it now what with all of the kids that sneak into the school at this hour out of a dare. It's actually funny when you think about it!"

Jason backed up a bit and asked, "So, you *are* a spirit? I'm not just seeing things?" After all, this was where it all started for him, seeing spirits that no one else could see.

"Yes." She giggled. "Now, if you don't mind, could you please help me with something?" the girl asked.

CHAPTER 11

"**A**nything?" Kalen asked as she met up with Gage on the second floor.

"Nada? You?" Gage replied.

"Nothing. But I can still sense the energy. It has to be here somewhere. I hope Jason is okay."

"Yeah, where *is* Jason?"

"You mean you don't know? I thought you'd run into him on the way down." Kalen shot him an exasperated look.

"Uh, I assumed you were keeping tabs on him."

Kalen turned to him, her green eyes ablaze with fury. "You *suck* sometimes, you know that?!"

Gage's piercing blue eyes widened in disbelief. "Well, excuse me for not being Jason!" He threw his hands up mockingly.

"Wh-what the hell's your problem? When did I ever compare you to Jason?" Kalen marched in front of him, her eyes shrinking to a dubious squint.

"Well, to say that I 'suck' implies that there's someone *better* to compare me to! Someone like *Jason,* maybe," Gage hissed.

Kalen rolled her eyes and turned her back to

him, arms crossed. She huffed and stormed off hurriedly, and Gage awkwardly followed behind her.

Something black appeared in her line of sight. Kalen jumped back.

"Kalen, what's wrong?"

"Look at that wall over there," she replied, her posture suddenly on the defensive.

Gage looked to the wall she had pointed to. Some kind of black animal appendage was sticking out of the wall. The pair backed away as the creature shot through the wall and came straight at them.

*   *   *

"What do you need help with?" Jason asked the ghost girl, sitting on the ground.

The ghost girl sat close to him, clinging to him almost in a childlike manner, and replied, "You see …"

Bang!

Boom!

"Ahhh!!" the ghost girl screamed, hugging Jason tightly. "*That!*"

"What?" Jason asked. "And what was that noise?"

"I know what it was! Follow me! Your friends are in danger!" said the ghost girl, who floated quickly out of the bathroom, Jason following closely behind.

Once down the stairs, he saw a giant lizard-like monster, with ten legs and a long skull on its head. It charged at Kalen, who had already readied her weapon. She jumped out of the way of her adversary, then sliced upward and spun, gracefully as usual. The beast screeched loudly and then whipped its tail at her, sending her flying and slamming her into the wall with a hard thud!

"Kalen! I'm coming!" Jason said, running over to her. He crouched over her protectively when the monster struck him with his tail.

"Jason!" Kalen cried out.

"I'm fine! I'm gonna get this guy!" Jason said determinedly.

"No, you *idiot!* It's too strong to fight *alone!* Where's Gage?" Kalen shouted.

Jason aimed his arrow at the monster's head. He held his bow steady, then as he was about to launch the arrow, the monster turned around and charged at him, making him flinch.

"*Gotcha*!" someone called out.

Just then, a white blast of energy slammed into the creature. It was Gage's Spirit Energy bullets! Gage jumped in front of the monster and kicked it in the mouth, sending it staggering backwards. It screeched in pain again and opened its mouth wide, trying to eat Gage whole! Jason was too shocked to move. But Gage grabbed its large, sharp teeth and lifted it up to the ceiling. Then, his Spirit Energy fired from his hands, sending the beast flying. The beast got up again, but this time pieces of it were blasted off by Gage's energy blast.

"Whew! This is gonna be a tough one!" Gage said, wiping sweat from his brows.

"Yeah …" Jason groaned.

"Couldn't ask for better!" Gage said with a smirk.

"You're actually getting a kick out of this?!" Jason exclaimed.

Before Jason could get a straight answer out of him, he noticed that Gage's posture was slumping and his moves got more sluggish with each attack. His power consumed a lot of Spirit Energy apparently.

*   *   *

Beatrice stood in front of Samson Manor, staring at the moon.

I hope Gage and the others are okay, she thought.

This was pretty much the routine every time Gage set out for a mission. First, he would rush out the door, window, or whatever the closest exit was, yelling, "See ya, Trix! I'm off to destroy another one! Be back in time for dinner!" Then, Beatrice spent the rest of the time wondering how hard it was for him to go off and "destroy another one."

She wondered if he was badly hurt, if he was hungry, hot, or cold, or if he ever felt really scared while he was fighting. She wanted so badly to be able to go with him, make herself useful. But whenever she insisted, he looked at her like she was insane and replied, "No way, it's too dangerous. You need to stay here where it's safe. It *is* my job as your new big brother to make sure that you are." Then, she would spend the rest of the evening in the apartment doing whatever menial task she could to keep her mind occupied.

And when he came home, she would be waiting at the door to greet him, fighting back the tears of relief over the fact that he was home and in one piece. She wanted nothing more than to help in any way that she could. It was the least she could do for everything he and his family had done for her. And that was when she decided that *tonight* was the night she was going to do it.

*   *   *

"Man! This guy won't let up!" Jason complained, panting.

"Yeah! Even I'm getting tired!" Gage huffed.

"All we've been doing so far is firing at it

randomly. We need to come up with a plan!" said Kalen.

The three teens were bent over in exhaustion, hiding in the janitor's closet. They had been fighting the monster for over an hour. "Well, on the bright side, it looks like Spider-zilla over there is getting tired, too," said Jason, peaking out.

"*Spider-zilla?*" Gage repeated dubiously. "*That's* the best name you could come up with?"

"You got a better one?" Jason asked flatly.

"Well … no, not really … Anyway, Kalen's right; we have to come up with some kind of strategy," said Gage.

"Okay, how about this? First, I charge in and strike at him from several sides so he only focuses on me. Then, *you*, Gage, will fire your bullets at him. Then, lastly, while we do that, *you*, Jason, will aim for the monster's stomach," said Kalen.

Then she looked around, Jason nowhere to be found. Gage cleared his throat, and then pointed behind her, where Jason was already charging at the monster, bow and arrow in hand. At first, Kalen smiled, watching Jason bravely charge into the fight like a true warrior, but then she snapped out of it and yelled, "You idiot! Did you listen to a word I said?!"

"Doesn't look like it!" Gage chuckled.

"Quiet you!" Kalen growled.

"Okay! Geez," Gage said.

Jason knew he should have listened to Kalen's strategy, but something in him made him charge at the monster impulsively. Maybe it was bravery. Maybe it was the Moderator in him. Maybe he just didn't want to risk having Gage show him up again. Either way, he was in front of the monster and it was *mad*. He felt as though Death were staring him in the face. Again, his courage was failing him. He was suddenly so frightened he couldn't move. One of the monster's arms swung right at him. He closed his eyes and hoped that the blow wouldn't be too painful. He heard a crunching sound. He opened one eye and saw a big blue barrier in front of him. Then behind the barrier, he caught a glimpse of blonde hair.

"*Beatrice?!*" Jason cried incredulously.

Gage and Kalen were as shocked as he was. "Wh-what are you doing here, Beatrice?!" Kalen cried out. Gage stood speechless, with a look of not only shock, but *terror*. "Get back to the others, Jason! I don't know how much longer I can—" said Beatrice.

She let out a scream after her barrier was blown away by the monster's fist. She fell to the ground on her back and slid. "No! Bea!" Gage screamed, running to her frantically.

"I-I can't believe you came here! I told you it was still too dangerous for you!" Gage scolded her, while carrying her away from the fray.

"I just wanted to … I just wanted to …!" Beatrice struggled to say with all of the pain that she was in.

"Well, you shouldn't have! Look at you!" Gage scolded, looking down at her bruised forehead.

Jason watched as Beatrice hung her head down, tears of shame dripping from her light green eyes. Then Gage smiled and stroked his fingers in her hair and said, "There, there. No more crying now … I'll explain it to them later … Okay?"

"Okay …," Beatrice replied. As she wiped the tears from her eyes, Jason turned his attention back to the monster.

Kalen charged at it, did a jumping somersault atop the monster's head, and then stabbed in on the crown. Then Gage tore away from Beatrice, jumped in front of the monster, fired one large blast of the last of his Spirit Energy, and the monster exploded. The blast was so strong, it sent the four of them flying to the end of the hallway.

All of them stumbled onto their feet, moaning and clutching their wounds.

Gage rolled over to Kalen, caressing her head, and asked with a smirk, "Do I 'suck' *now*?"

"You're such an ass," Kalen growled.

CHAPTER 12

Kalen shot up from the floor, then walked over to Jason, grabbed him by the collar, and shook him violently.

"You *idiot*!! Why did you go rushing off like that?! I thought we were going to plan a strategy! Huh?! *Remember*? What the hell happened back there?" she shrieked with fury.

"Okay, okay! I'm sorry! I just thought …" Jason tried to explain himself as he was being shaken. Kalen stopped shaking him and sighed.

Then she said more calmly, "Next time don't just go running off. It's just the three of us; we have to work together."

"Thank you very much for getting rid of that monster," the ghost girl said shyly.

"You're welcome," Beatrice replied sweetly from her position on the floor.

"You're right. We're a team, so we have to act like it," Jason said determinedly.

"Ugh! I think I'm gonna barf!" Gage complained, sticking his finger down his throat and making a fake gagging noise.

"Oh, shut up!" Jason said. Why did Gage always have to ruin everything?

Then Gage gave him a death glare and Jason recoiled, which resulted in Kalen glaring at Gage until he turned back around and continued to tend to Beatrice.

As he did, Jason noticed something different in Gage's posture. He was slouching and very pale and was panting more heavily than the rest of them. Maybe he just got carried away and used up too much of his Spirit Energy. He seemed like the type. Maybe he just needed a rest.

"Come on. Let's go home," Gage suddenly said to Beatrice.

"Right," she complied.

Just as they were about to teleport, Kalen yelled, "Hold on, you two! We're going with you!"

"Wh-why? What do you care? Don't you two *lovebirds* want some time alone together?" Gage asked bitterly.

Jason blushed and stepped away from Kalen as she did the same.

"It's not like that!" Kalen said, embarrassed. "Besides, Gage, I thought you'd appreciate the company."

"Well, now's not a good time," Gage replied.

Then Kalen put her stretched-out hands in front of her and said, "Okay, fine then. We'll back off for now."

"Yeah, call us when you're in a better mood.

Sheesh ...," Jason added, unable to keep the bitterness from his voice.

And with that Gage and Beatrice teleported to the Samson Manor.

Suddenly, Kalen grabbed Jason's hand and said, "Don't get any ideas. I'm just going to Gage's house to make sure they're okay and *you're* going to help me!"

Why this sudden concern for the jerk all of a sudden? Jason thought to himself. Out loud, he said, "Are you sure you're not being just a little paranoid? ... Or, are you sure you're not ... jealous or something?"

Kalen turned red and said indignantly, "Of course not! What are you thinking?! Why would I be jealous of those two? They're technically siblings! Don't think such dumb things!"

"Whatever you say ..."

*   *   *

After they teleported to the house, Gage carried Beatrice on his back and tiptoed up the stairs. He made sure to be very quiet—if his foster parents found out what had happened with Beatrice, they would kill him. As he reached the top of the steps, he heard footsteps. He rushed to his room, but was suddenly stopped by two tall figures.

One of them shouted, "Where have you two

been?! And why is Beatrice all battered and bruised?!"

"Jess, calm down. I'm sure they have an explanation for this," said the other one. Gage switched the lights on and saw Jessica and James standing in the hallway, arms crossed.

"I can explain …" Gage chuckled nervously.

"Better start," Jessica said, bitterly echoing Gage's tone.

Then Beatrice stepped in front of Gage and said, "*I'll* explain. Jessica, I went after Gage when he was out looking for a tainted spirit at the school. I'm sorry. I just wanted to help him … I just want to be of some use. It's the least I could have done for all of the protection you've all given me …"

The adult couple gave acknowledging smiles. "Aww, it's sweet of you to want to help, but you still need more training. Go to bed and get some rest, Beatrice," said Jessica.

Gage set Beatrice down and she walked down the hallway to her bedroom. When she walked into her room and shut the door, *thwack!*

"How could you let Beatrice do that?!" Jessica snapped at Gage, smacking him lightly on the back of the head.

"I know, I'm sorry. It won't happen again," Gage replied sincerely.

Then Jessica, looking guilty, put her hand to

his head and said, much more calmly, "You look exhausted. Go wash up and get some rest. You have school in the morning."

"Okay." Gage smiled, rubbing the back of his head. With that, Gage, Jessica, and James walked to their rooms to go to sleep.

*   *   *

Jason and Kalen, hidden under the elaborate, twisting stairs, overheard the entire conversation.

"So … Beatrice is a Moderator, too, huh?" Jason whispered.

"No shit," Kalen snarked. "But her powers seem to be defensive, not offensive like ours, so I'm guessing the Samsons don't like throwing her into fights."

Suddenly, he felt a hostile presence lurking behind him. He shivered and turned around.

"So that's what I was hearing this whole time … a pair of eavesdropping flies on the wall … when I *specifically* told them to go home!" Gage growled. "God! Why is no one listening to a *damn* word I say anymore?"

"Sorry, Gage! We were worried about you!" Kalen pleaded.

He let out an exasperated sigh and told them, "Follow me. I'll explain everything in the lounge."

The lounge was furnished with big leather couches. Gage flopped onto one of them and sighed wearily, "Whew! What a night. I'm wiped out!"

"That makes three of us." Kalen sighed.

"So, you and Beatrice aren't biological siblings, right?" Jason asked, trying to piece it all together.

"What do *you* think, genius?" Gage answered, pointing at his clearly Asian—and clearly irritated—face. "Yep. We ran into Beatrice at that store all those years back. Remember Kalen?"

Kalen nodded. "We first met Beatrice one day, about four or five years ago, when we saw her loitering in this cute tea shop. We left just after she did and saw that she was being harassed by this pervert. He was following her and saying all this gross suff. Gage and I stepped in between them and stood up for her."

"Right. She said she was on her way to a relative's house and had gotten lost"—Gage let out a chuckle—"Yeah, turns out that was a big fat lie. We took her back to the tea shop and it all came out. She was running away from her own family. From what Bea told me, they were hella abusive. I had only started living here recently, but when I found out, I just brought her over here to collect herself."

Jason furrowed his brow. "You just brought a cute girl, lost in the streets, over to your luxury apartment, to collect herself?"

Gage snapped back at him, "Duh! Like I was gonna leave 'a cute girl lost in the streets' all alone! Then, we got close, and I begged Jessica and James to let her live here."

Jason raised his eyebrows again but quickly lowered them so as not to earn Gage's wrath again.

"Long story short, they pulled a few strings, went through basically the same adoption process with Beatrice that they had with me, and the rest is history."

"And she's a Moderator?" asked Kalen.

"Sort of. Jessica and James saw that she had potential, but we want to keep it reigned in for now … because of all she's been through already."

"What about Amelia and Sandro?" Jason asked.

Kalen and Gage shook their heads. "Nope. Not Moderators. They no nothing," Gage said.

Then the chime of the clock rang through the room and Kalen said, "Well, it's getting late; we should all get some sleep. "We do have school in the morning."

"Let's try to get in as much pillow action as we can," said Gage.

Kalen shot him a look and then threw a pillow at him. Hard. Girl could've dominated the softball team, too. She had a hell of a throwing arm.

"What? I meant *sleep*!" Gage retorted. "The hell were you thinking I meant? Hmm?"

Kalen immediately dropped her suspicious look and went slightly pink in the face, as Gage chuckled smugly.

*   *   *

Kalen woke up the next morning exhausted. Once she got to school, she met up with the others. They were slumped on their lockers, with dark circles under their eyes, looking like zombies. Then Sandro and Amelia walked over and waved to the group.

"Hey guys!" said Amelia.

"What's going on?" said Sandro.

"Hey," they all groaned.

"What happened to you guys?" asked Amelia.

"We were up really late last night studying," said Kalen.

"You mean like a study group?" asked Sandro.

"And *Gage* was studying *with* you?" Amelia asked cynically, pointing at a yawning, droopy-eyed Gage.

Then, picking up on this little dig, Gage said, "Hey! What's so hard to believe about *that*?!"

"What were you guys really doing?" Amelia asked teasingly.

"We meant what we said! We were just

studying too long," said Jason, who Amelia and Sandro had already accepted into the group—knowing nothing about the other group he'd been accepted into.

Amelia walked towards him, giving him a hard, suspicious glare, startling him and making him hide behind Beatrice.

"It's true!" Beatrice smiled.

"Well, I can't mistrust you, Trix, so it must be true!" Amelia smiled.

Just then, the bell rang and a sea of students moved through the halls like fish swimming up a stream.

"Hey, we should get to our class now, guys!" said Sandro. "*Let go! Let go!*"

"For the hundredth time, Sandro, it's *let's* go!"

*   *   *

Long after the buzz of the students shuffling through the halls and classrooms filling up, a pretty but plain-looking girl with long black hair stood behind at her locker. She let out a tight exhale and rubbed her temples.

Breathe in. Breathe out. Just like the counselor told me.

Unbeknownst to her, a pocket of black mist surrounded her with each breath she took. Her feet dragged as though they were bound to boulders as she stepped down the halls.

God, I hate being in school ... I can't take it anymore ...

As soon as that thought manifested in her mind, the back mist intensified and enveloped her.

*   *   *

At lunchtime, the group sat at a table by the window. Jason had tried to flag Dimitria over but she stayed where she was. Kalen turned to the others and said, "Something's been bothering me about last night."

"What is it?" Jason asked. It must be serious if it bothered Kalen. She was made of steel.

"These Shadowmonsters have been showing up a lot lately. First, it was the Shadowmonster at the movies. Then, there was that centipede one, then the lizard one, and then there was that Shadowmonster at the school," said Kalen.

"Now that ya mention it, these things have been showin' up a lot lately," said Gage.

"It's been worrying me, too," said Beatrice.

"Whoever, or whatever, it is that's creating these things might be targeting us. They might even be somewhere nearby," said Kalen.

"Yeah, maybe," said Jason, as his palms went damp. This is exactly why he was hesitant to join the Moderators, even if they hadn't turned out to be a crazy cult.

CHAPTER 13

Black mist seeped through the hallways of Whitewood High. Kalen, Jason and Gage could feel it as though it were a thick smoke.

Jason gagged and said, "Ugh, it's like there's a gas leak in here."

"Yeah. It's the essence of some kind of Shadowmonster. A really strong one, I'm betting," said Kalen.

"So, this means more ghost ass-kicking, right?" Gage popped up from the side and grinned.

"Yes, Gage. We're going to be doing more ghost ass-kicking," Kalen replied coolly. "I don't know when, but were definitely doing more ass-kicking today."

They walked down the halls to their art class, which conveniently had the window with the best view of the front lawn. Jason looked out the window where there was a large, orange oak tree in the grassy field. Groups of students sat under it, giggling and chattering happily. Despite the presence of the supernatural, these students, unsuspecting, were so carefree, creating an atmosphere of bliss that surrounded the place.

Suddenly, a voice snapped at him, "Mr.

Walker! Quit your daydreaming and get into your seat! Class is about to start!"

Jason's body whipped back to the man in the glasses behind him. He said to the teacher, "Yes, Mr. Parker."

He sat next to Kalen and Gage, the first smiling acceptingly, the second rolling his eyes and looking down at his sketchbook.

Mr. Parker went up to the front of the classroom and said, "For today's class you may go draw *whatever you want*! Even … *me*!" Mr. Parker ran his fingers through his short, brown hair.

"Kidding!" he interjected. "*Only* kidding! Have fun, class!"

Kalen slapped her hand onto her forehead, shaking her head. The rest of the class exchanged equally uncomfortable glances.

"I know who *my* muse is gonna be!" Gage raised a seductive eyebrow and slid over to an attractive male classmate sitting in front of him.

"Gage, quit screwing around! Let's go find something else to draw!" Kalen pulled Gage's ear angrily, making him grimace.

"Ow! Kalen, that hurts! Come on, stop!" he complained.

"*You* stop being an *idiot*!" said Kalen.

"But … but … I need to express myself through my *art*!" he shouted melodramatically as the three of them walked out the door.

"Shut up! Seriously, do you have *any* sense of modesty?" Kalen shouted, punching him in the arm.

When they walked outside the school, Jason walked over to the oak tree he'd admired earlier and muttered to himself, "That's such a beautiful tree. If only there were something I could draw with it."

Kalen, standing right next to him, heard what he had said and stared at him with a "What an idiot" look on her face for a moment.

She stood in front of him and said, "Hey! Thinking of something to draw? You know, if I could make a suggestion, you could draw someone you know …"

Jason blushed and said, "Umm … y-yeah … Oh, I know! I could draw you! I-if you don't mind …"

Kalen smiled and said, "No. I don't mind at all …"

"Then let's go over there," said Jason, pointing to the oak tree.

They discussed their ideas for a while, and decided they would draw each other. Jason went first and the work went quickly.

"I'm almost done. Just hold on a little longer," Jason said by the end of his sketch, "Then, it'll be your turn to draw me!"

Suddenly Kalen turned bright red.

"Um, Jason? Promise you won't judge me?"

asked Kalen.

Jason said, "I would never judge you, Kalen. I think you're perfect." Then they both went red.

"Well, I'm not exactly the best at drawing … Actually, I'm terrible at it …," Kalen said in embarrassment, then barked at him, "D-don't you *dare* laugh if it doesn't come out well, got it?!"

Jason chuckled and then quickly thought better of it. Then he said sweetly, "I don't care how it looks; it's the thought that counts, right?"

He held up his picture of her and she blushed an even deeper red. He knew he was a decent artist, and he swelled with pride as he could tell she liked his sketch of her. Though he didn't think it did her justice by half.

*　　*　　*

Meanwhile, in his office, Moros was staring into his reflection in a compact mirror vainly. He chuckled and thought about a girl with long black hair who had come to talk to him just a few minutes ago. Her name was Evelyn Sawyer. She was a senior and honor's student who was very stressed about doing well on the SAT, and she was not sleeping well at night. He had told her kindly to try to take her mind off of it for a while and take a break when she could. She thanked him politely and left.

"That girl was potent with dark energy. She will be perfect for what I have planned next," he muttered to himself.

*   *   *

On the other side of the yard from Kalen and Jason, Gage was walking up and asking cute girls and guys if he could sketch them. Each time they shook their heads and walked away, he could see Kalen laughing and shaking her head at him.

Another potential target! "Hey there, sweet thing!" Gage said flirtatiously to a pretty senior girl. "I'm looking for a muse and I think you might be her."

The girl put her long black hair behind her ears and said, "Sure."

She followed Gage to the stairs by the front entrance and sat on the steps. Then Gage couldn't help but notice that the girl looked a little anemic.

"You okay? You seem a little tired," he said to the girl.

"Oh, I'm fine. Don't worry about me," the girl said, smiling somewhat weakly.

Gage pulled out his sketchbook and pencil and started sketching. Suddenly, black smoke appeared around Gage and the girl. Gage stopped sketching a moment to watch the smoke swirling. He coughed. The girl sat on the steps unaware.

"What's wrong?" she asked, "Why are you coughing?"

"Nothing. I just caught a little bug, that's all. I guess there's something going around," Gage said, smiling.

Very quickly, the smoke got thicker and more overwhelming, and Gage coughed harder. He thought about flagging Kalen over, but she was busy with her little lover boy.

"Gage, are you sure you're okay?" the girl asked.

"Yeah, I'm sure," said Gage, still coughing.

Then, the smoke travelled closer to the black-haired girl. She inhaled and the smoke seemed to go inside of her. Then she began to cough.

"You alright?" Gage asked her.

"Do you smell that?" she asked him, then coughed again. Now she was coughing worse than he was.

*   *   *

Moros, I require more human souls ...

"Patience, patience," said Moros.

That last girl you absorbed, what do you plan to do with her?

"Girl? Oh, I plan to use her as bait. I've infected her with your energy, and soon she will become one of ours. That is, if those children don't get to her first," said Moros.

"I must go, Master, and see to your plan."

*   *   *

Evelyn collapsed onto the side of the stairs.

"Hey!" Gage yelled to her. He rushed over to Evelyn, who was now coughing in agony as the black smoke engulfed her entire body. Gage grabbed her by the shirt collar and shook her repeatedly. When she lifted her head up, Gage recoiled in horror as her once sallow, soft face was now completely white and the contours of her face more hardened, hollowed out, and threatening.

The girl opened her eyes abruptly. The expression on her face went from soft and gentle to deadly, violent, and unhinged. Then the girl opened her mouth and began to laugh hysterically. In a jolt of surprise, Gage shoved her to the ground and backed away.

The girl lay there in silence for several seconds when suddenly her shoulder shot up to the sky, and then her arm. She then flung out the other arm and slowly rag-dolled up to her feet taking a raspy, labored breath with each movement.

Gage summoned a pair of Spirit Energy guns from his hands and braced into a fighting stance as the possessed girl suddenly grew long claws and charged at him.

CHAPTER 14

Jason noticed the commotion from afar and turned to Kalen. "What's going on over there?" Students stood in clumps, blocking the view.

Kalen held out her hands and the black sun mark expanded on the back of her palms as she scanned their surroundings for an energy source. "There's a huge wave of supernatural energy coming from over there."

"Let's go check it out!"

*   *   *

Gage braced himself, gripping his dual handguns tightly, jumping away from the now possessed black-haired girl's furious slashes. The girl jumped up high and then kicked Gage in the face. Gage fell on his back, then swept his leg under one of the girl's, tripping her. She got up quickly, swung her claw at him, and cut him on the cheek.

Then the second claw swung at him, and he intercepted it with one handgun and fired on her with the other. He shot at her multiple times, her body jerking back at every Energy Bullet that hit her. He stopped firing at her and backed away from the girl's body. He readied his gun for another blast when he jumped at the sound of an amused chuckle.

As the possessed girl moved to sit up, the chuckling escalated into menacing, violent laughter. The girl got up to her feet and started to tilt her head to the left. Gage recoiled as the girl's head tilted so far that her chin was right her forehead would have been. Her head had flipped *upside down*! She held up her claws and charged at Gage, laughing hysterically with her head upside down.

*   *   *

"I can sense the immense Spirit Energy coming from outside. From the marksman and the girl, and the other two are making their way there. It looks like all of our problems will be solved in just a moment," said Moros.

Which is good, since I have to get a haircut at 5:00, he thought.

I can read your thoughts, you know ..., the black entity said in Moros's mind.

Whoops! He he. Sorry, Master, Moros apologized.

Moros got up from his chair, grabbed a set of keys that was lying on his desk, and locked his door with them. A short man in a suit and a bright striped tie came up to him and asked, "Where are you going so early?"

"I'm going to the salon. That is a *great* tie,

by the way!" Moros replied with a smug smile.

"Why, thank you!" said the short man.

"Take care!" Moros said, walking out the door.

"That was the most *horrific-looking* tie I've ever seen!" Moros muttered under his breath.

*   *   *

Gage grabbed the ghoul by the hair and put a Spirit Energy gun to her head. "I'm sorry to have to do this. But after I'm done with this, your soul will go to a better place," he whispered in her ear as she struggled. "And you were such a cutie, too," he said. He readied his gun when Kalen suddenly appeared in front of him. *Ow!* She'd kicked him in the stomach, sending him flying into a nearby tree!

The Shadowmonster slashed at her, scratching her uniform. She kicked the monster in the face and ran over to Gage.

"What do you think you're doing?!" she yelled. Jason stood behind her.

"What are *you* doing?! She was possessed by some dark energy, grew claws, and started attacking me!" Gage explained.

"She's a living *human* that turned into a *Shadowmonster*! What we need to do is get her to a Healer! *Fast*!" said Kalen.

"But what if we're too late?" asked Gage.

"Maybe they can exorcise her! It's worth a try!" said Kalen.

"Okay, fine. Just one thing," said Gage.

"Yeah?" asked Kalen.

"We can't take her anywhere if she's *trying to kill us*!" Gage cried, pointing to the girl running over to them, head still upside down, claws slashing about.

The girl's body suddenly radiated an intense black aura.

"Did you see that?" Gage cried. "That's the same kind of energy we see in the Shadowmonsters we usually fight! Kalen, I don't think we're going to be able to—"

Suddenly someone appeared before them that they were not expecting.

"Jess!" Gage gasped.

"We need your help! This girl ..." Kalen started to say.

"I know. I saw it all. I can still sense the humanity in her. She's possessed and going to need a Healer now, isn't she?" Jessica smiled. "You guys help me hold her still and then I'll take her off your hands."

"Thank you." Kalen sighed.

"No problem." Jessica turned to the possessed girl and then turned to Gage. "Gage, aim for the girl's head. Don't worry; it won't affect her directly, just the monster inside her."

"On it!" said Gage, who had already summoned a giant bazooka made of Spirit Energy.

"No, no, no! That's too much! Just use your handguns!" Jessica said frantically.

"That's what I'm always telling him," yelled Kalen.

"Okay, okay!" Gage said, changing his weapon back into a handgun. He focused on the girl, who had been running around in circles all this time. When she saw him, she sped off across the street.

"Oh no, you don't!" Gage yelled. He teleported in front of her, aimed for her head, and held her writhing body down on the ground.

The girl screamed angrily and struggled as Jessica and the others rushed over. Then Jessica grabbed the girl and suddenly her body and the girl's body started to teleport away. "You guys go back to school; I'll handle this one!" Jessica smiled.

"O-okay then …," Gage said warily. He and Kalen walked away from the woman and dragged a dejected Jason along with them.

The three of them were making their way under one of the trees when Gage sat up and panicked. "Aw, crap! Now that that girl's gone, I gotta find another muse! And there's only another half hour left! Damn! See ya later, guys!" and with that he sped off, looking for something else to draw.

*   *   *

A half hour later, the students walked back into the art room and sat in their desks. Jason slumped onto his desk sadly. Once again, Jason couldn't do anything to help.

Damn! What's wrong with me? I couldn't do anything. Again. I let myself get shown up by Gage ... Again! Kalen was right before. I need more training, if I'm cut out for this at all.

Just then, Mr. Parker walked into the classroom and said happily, "Well, class! I hope all of you finished sketching! Everyone, come up one at a time and show the class what you drew!"

The first to come up was Jason. He opened up a page in his sketchbook and in it was a sketch of Kalen smiling under a giant oak tree.

"Ooh! How beautiful! B+!" said Mr. Parker.

"Thanks, Mr. Parker!" Jason smiled. When Jason went back to his seat, Gage looked at him with a small smirk.

"Alright, who's next?" asked Mr. Parker.

A girl with short brown hair walked up to the front of the class and pulled out a picture of a rosebush from the schoolyard.

"Beautiful! B+ for you as well!" said Mr. Parker, "Gage! Wouldn't you like to come up next?"

"Huh? Well, okay then ..." Gage blushed, which was not his style.

He got up to the front of the class and opened his sketchbook shyly. Jason and Kalen looked on curiously. Gage had just recently transferred into this art class from another class due to a schedule mix-up, so they hadn't seen any drawings from him. On the newest page of his sketchbook was a picture of Beatrice with a sweet, gentle look on her face. The sketch appeared almost life-like, and the whole classroom was agape.

Mr. Parker gasped in ecstasy and said, "Oh my! This is … this is … *amazing*! So life-like! So spectacular! From the look on her face to that spark of innocence and purity, it's all so wonderful! If I didn't know any better, I'd swear this girl were a princess smiling from her castle!"

That last comment made Gage, Kalen, and Jason hold back a chuckle.

"A+!" said Mr. Parker, making Gage blush heavily and give a small smile.

Wow … Never would've pegged him for the artistic type, thought Jason.

"Oh my. Would you look at the time? We only have time for one last sketch. So, who is going to show us their magnificent masterpiece this time? Kalen?"

This time it was Kalen's turn to blush as she got up and held her sketchbook gingerly. She opened it and turned to her sketch of Jason. The class went silent with blank stares.

"Oh … oh my …" Mr. Parker said.

The drawing was stringy and cartoonish, but Jason liked it. Then a few students sitting in the far back started snickering.

Kalen stood awkwardly in front of the class, not moving or speaking. She was either frozen from embarrassment or lost in the haze of some bad memory or another.

"A-!" Mr. Parker cried with joy.

Kalen's face lit up with a mix of relief and surprise. "It's so avant-garde and surreal! This is *art*! It need not necessarily be a realistic depiction of the human anatomy; it only need be about what you feel! There is no *perfection* in art!" said Mr. Parker.

Jason and Gage smiled at Kalen and gave her encouraging winks and thumbs-up. Kalen's body suddenly looked a bit lighter, as though some sort of weight had lifted from her shoulders.

When the bell rang, everyone left the classroom. As they were walking down the halls, Jason teased, "Wow, Gage! Never would've pegged you as the artistic type!"

Gage nervously began to fidget with the strings on his jacket. "Well … I … you know…," he said anxiously.

Then Kalen said sweetly, "You did a great job! How come you never told me you were so talented?"

That made Gage smile.

"I-I don't know … It's not that big of a deal!" he said modestly. Kalen patted him on the back and the three of them walked down a flight of stairs. Whatever awkwardness had come up between Kalen and Gage seemed to have resolved itself, which, despite the fact that he still wasn't sure about Gage, made him glad.

*   *   *

"Moros! They took the girl into the other world! They are going to exorcise her! How are you planning to fix this?" said Moros's disembodied master.

"Don't worry, Master. It has been in her system long enough to make an exorcism futile. Worst case scenario, she will no longer be human by the time they prepare the exorcism and either she will kill them or they will have to kill her," Moros said almost coldly. "Our tracks will be completely covered."

"I see … Well, Moros, we must harvest more souls, and this time, make sure those Moderators do not get in the way …"

"Yes, Master," said Moros.

*   *   *

It was the end of the school day and the Moderators were crossing the street on their way to the subway.

On the way to the platform, Jason turned to Kalen and said, "Um, Kalen? I need to tell you something …"

Kalen blushed and gave him a confused look, asking, "Wh-what would *that* be, Jason?"

"Yeah, what would *that* be, Jason?" Gage echoed Kalen's question in an angrier tone.

"I want to start training in earnest!" Jason said surprisingly boldly.

"Oh … Well, sure Jason," Kalen replied, somewhat disappointed. "We can go to my place!"

"Oh no! We're going to *my* place!" Gage declared forcefully. Everyone turned to Gage and gave him shocked looks.

"W-well, that's nice of you, Gage!" Beatrice said softly.

"Um, yeah. And unexpected … but yeah! We'll go to your place! Thanks!" Jason said appreciatively.

Kalen looked at Gage suspiciously, but then agreed. "Sure! Thank you! I hope it isn't an imposition!"

"No, no! It's no imposition at all!"

Gage fanned his hand at her modestly, then pounded one fist into his other hand and said, "It's about time somebody *properly* showed this rookie the ropes!"

Jason gulped at this gesture, but then smirked and said, "You're on!"

Gage chuckled, went over to his rival, put one hand on his shoulder and said, "You're so in over your head, kid, you don't even know it."

Kalen rushed in between, pushed the two boys apart, and said, "Break it up, boys! Save it for the training session!"

Then Beatrice shyly chimed in, "Um, Gage? I'd like to train, too, if that's okay."

Gage stared at his friend's blushing face and said, "Aww! How can I say no to an adorable face like that? Okay, but …"

"I can spar with her while you and Jason have your little sparring match. How's that sound?" Kalen said.

"Uh … but…," Gage stuttered.

"Don't worry! I'll go easy on her if that'll help you sleep at night!" Kalen teased.

"A-alright then! W-wait a minute! I-it's not like—! I'm not worried about her in *that* way!" Gage snapped.

Kalen laughed at this while Beatrice giggled.

Kalen patted him on the back and said chuckling, "Alright, alright! Calm down, you big lug! Let's get on the train, already!"

CHAPTER 15

So, I'm back in the Realm of the Moderators. Jason thought. *And in the training grounds.*

The sky above him was a dark red and the clouds were a heavy gray. The trees surrounding the field were wilted and dead, and the air smelled like rust.

"Why does it look like this anyway?" he asked.

"This place is like this because of the effects of the Outbreak on this world. The Shadowmonsters are deteriorating this realm with that dark aura of theirs," said Kalen.

Just over the horizon, Jason caught a faint glimpse of something thin protruding from one of the red, sandy hills. "What's that over there?" he asked, pointing towards said hill.

"Those are tombstones … of the many Moderators who were killed in battle," Kalen responded brusquely.

"That's terrible," said Jason.

Kalen nodded. "Did you know that a portion of those deaths were caused by possession via Shadowmonster? That they lost control over their own bodies and started attacking their comrades?

That they were killed knowing there was an opportunity, albeit small, to cure them?"

The rest of the group, even Gage, winced. "Yeesh, that's even worse," Jason said.

Gage mumbled. "It's just like the girl from earlier…"

"All of those Moderators who believed that they had no choice but to kill one of their own …," said Beatrice quietly.

"If we train hard enough, we'll get rid of every last one of those bastards!" Gage boasted, apparently trying to break the tension.

"Yeah," Jason said weakly.

"Yeah!" Beatrice smiled.

Kalen remained silent, then turned to Beatrice. "You ready to do this, Trix?"

"Yeah," Beatrice said again, smiling wider.

"Yeah, yeah, let's get to it then!" Gage urged, a Spirit Energy handgun already in hand.

"Yeah! Let's do this! I'll give it everything I've got!" said Jason.

I have to. I'm not gonna get shown up again!

Gage led him away from the girls and suddenly a giant white screen appeared. Then a black vortex surged inside the white screen and spun like a whirlpool in it. "I'm gonna take you somewhere where we won't bother the little ladies here."

Kalen let out a groan and sighed, "You don't need to worry about us. We can hold our own here."

"Still, we don't want to crash into one another while we're sparring, right?" Gage asked.

"Yeah, probably not," Kalen said hesitantly. Then she nodded and said, "Go on then."

And with that, Gage dragged Jason by the collar into the vortex. "Huh? W-wait a sec! Hey! Let go! Come on, Gage! Let go!" he cried as his body was dragged into the portal.

*   *   *

In a room dimly lit with candles circling the center, several hooded men knelt next to each one. In the center of the circle was the possessed black-haired girl, struggling to break free from the ropes tied to her arms as well as a large red sun symbol underneath her.

"How is she?" asked Jessica.

"Her condition is getting worse. If we don't act fast, she'll have completely lost her humanity," said a woman's voice. The woman speaking had a mask covering her mouth and her eyes were glowing silver.

The room tensed.

"Don't worry, we'll take care of things from here. She can be healed. I can sense it," said the woman.

"Okay …," said Jessica.

She sent Spirit Energy from her hands and created a large, glowing white portal in between two giant doors. On the top of the doors, there were words engraved on a plaque reading Hall of the Healers. Jessica stepped toward the portal.

I hope they can heal her in time, she thought.

The girl roared and writhed in a psychotic rage. A group of hooded Healers circled around the girl and began to chant words in Greek that Jessica was familiar with.

"Purge and Purify," they chanted.

"Purge and Purify ..."

"Purge and Purify ..."

The possessed girl roared at the hooded Healers as the Shadowmonster inside of her writhed inside of her. An elderly Healer lifted his hand over to her head and chanted again.

"Purge and Purify …"

This time the energy of Shadowmonster in the girl's body began to channel into the man's hand. It made the girl's eyes turn black and move up to the back of her head. A bulge appeared in the middle of her forehead.

"We're almost there!" said one of the hooded men.

"Yes! Keep going!" Then the dark energy appeared from outside of the girl's body. The man summoned a ball of Spirit Energy and it sucked in all of the mysterious dark energy. The girl stopped screaming and passed out. Suddenly, color began to flush back into the girl's body.

"The color is beginning to return to her," said the elder hooded man.

"Do you have any idea what this girl's name was?"

"I think her name was Evelyn. Evelyn Sawyer, an honor's student at my son's school," said Jessica.

"Well, it's a good thing she is alive, then. A lot of people would have been let down if she weren't, it would seem," one of the Healers said, and smiled.

Jessica smiled back, and turned for the portal. "Make sure she is returned home safely. That way, by the time she wakes up, she'll think all of this was just a very strange dream."

Jessica's expression retained a modicum of composure as she disappeared through the portal. Then, she walked down the hallway of her own home and did a little shimmy.

"This calls for a celebration … with *booze*!" she cheered.

As Jessica inched closer to the door, she felt a faint energy. A low murmur. She shrugged and kept walking. Then she felt it stronger, from inside the Healer's Room. She furrowed a brow and beelined back through the portal. What she stumbled into upon entering made her legs give way and let gravity weigh her down to the ground.

Healers, covered in blood, shrieking and hiding their faces in their hands in horror and shame.

The girl, huddled on the ground trembling with blood in her hands.

Jessica collected herself and walked over to the girl with a smile, desperately trying to hide the impending terror inside her.

"Are you okay there, sweetie? I know this has all been a lot for you."

The girl let out a low, pained groan, making Jessica jump back a bit.

She took out her hand and said, "Here, take my hand. We'll get you out of here, get you all cleaned up, and get you ho—!"

The girl looked up at her … or *was she still a girl*? Her eyes were teary, but devoid of life. Jessica tried to search them for any sort of light, hope, anything, but it was a fruitless search. Then Jessica's eyes panned down to the girl's neck. A knife was lodged halfway into it. Jessica could smell the blood on her neck beginning to rust and feel the blood inside her own body grow cold. She let out a shriek and turned to the Healers.

"Hey, tell me what happened here! Someone help her!"

No. *No.* She couldn't let it happen again. She couldn't. She. Just. Couldn't.

Acknowledgements

When I graduated from high school, I had come up with a brilliant idea for a debut stand-alone novel. All I had to do was write a story about four kids battling strange monsters in New York City. My eighteen-year-old self thought that I had it all figured out and that this project would be a bestseller by now.

Ha.

I did not have it all figured out. Not for a long damn time. In fact, the book you are holding in your hands is probably the tenth? ... eleventh? ... rewrite, revision, re-whatever of that story. And I've decided, for my own sanity, to break it down into more than one book. But on the bright side, after at least thirteen years of overthinking (and just life happening in general) slowing me down, it's finally finished.

I'd like to thank my parents, Dagmar and Claiton, my friends, my fiancé, Adam, the Squid Squad, and last but not least all of my beta readers for providing feedback, emotional support, ideas, and patience putting up with my immense indecision and self-consciousness during each hurdle through each process of getting this book done.

About the Author

Lilah Souza is a Brazilian-American writer from New York. She is a sci-fi and fantasy lover who has been weaving her daydreams and nightmares into all sorts of chilling and thrilling tales since she was five years old. She graduated with a Bachelor's in Psychology at Wagner College, a Master's in Mental Health Counseling at LIU Brooklyn, and studied film during her high school years at G-Star School of the Arts. When she's not writing, Lilah enjoys reading, painting, playing video games, or indulging in various shenanigans. Her debut short story collection, *Scrambled Eggs*, is available on Amazon, and her work has been featured in *Bullshit Lit*.

Follow Lilah's journey on Instagram @l33lzonwh33lz, Facebook at Lilah Souza, Author, or Bluesky @lsouzawrites.